Pleasure in Reading

WHAT THE NEIGHBOURS DID AND OTHER STORIES

Pleasure in Reading

HAT THE NEIGHBOURS DID AND OTHER STORIES

PHILIPPA PEARCE

Illustrated by Faith Jaques

Longman

LONGMAN GROUP LIMITED
London

*Associated companies, branches and
representatives throughout the world*

© 1959, 1967, 1969, 1972 by Philippa Pearce

This collection first published 1972 under the Longman Young
Books imprint now Kestrel Books

This edition first published by Longman Group Ltd 1977

"What the Neighbours Did" was first published in *Twentieth
Century*, First Quarter 1967, and subsequently adapted for
broadcasting in the BBC School Broadcasting series *Living
Language*; "Still Jim and Silent Jim" was first published in 1959
by Basil Blackwell and Mott Ltd.; "Return to Air" was
originally written for the BBC School Broadcasting series *Over
to You* in 1964, and was first published, in a slightly different
form, in *The Friday Miracle and other stories*, edited by Kaye Webb,
published in 1969 by Penguin Books Ltd.

ISBN 0 582 18038 4

*Printed in Hong Kong by
Sheck Wah Tong Printing Press*

To Martin

who read the first story

Contents

What the Neighbours Did

Mum didn't like the neighbours, although—as we were the end cottage of the row—we only had one, really: Dirty Dick. Beyond him, the Macys.

Dick lived by himself—they said there used to be a wife, but she'd run away years ago; so now he lived as he wanted, which Mum said was like a pig in a pig-sty. Once I told Mum that I envied him, and she blew me up for it. Anyway, I'd have liked some of the things he had. He had two cars, although not for driving. He kept rabbits in one, and hens roosted in the other. He sold the eggs, which made part of his living. He made the rest from dealing in old junk (and in the village they said that he'd a stocking full of gold sovereigns which he kept under the mattress of his bed). Mostly he went about on foot, with his handcart for the junk; but he also rode a tricycle. The boys used to jeer at him sometimes, and once I asked him why he didn't ride a bicycle like everyone else. He said he liked a tricycle because you could go as slowly as you wanted, looking at things properly, without ever falling off.

Mrs Macy didn't like Dirty Dick any more than my mum did, but then she disliked everybody anyway. She didn't like Mr Macy. He was retired, and every morning in all weathers Mrs Macy'd turn him out into the garden and lock the door against him and make him stay there until he'd done as much work as she thought right. She'd put his dinner out to him through the scullery window. She couldn't bear to have anything alive about the place (you couldn't count old Macy himself, Dad used to say). That was one of the reasons why she didn't think much of us, with our dog and cat and Nora's two love-birds in a cage. Dirty Dick's hens and rabbits were even worse, of course.

Then the affair of the yellow dog made the Macys really hate Dirty Dick. It seems that old Mr Macy secretly got himself a dog. He never had any money of his own, because his wife made him hand it over, every week; so Dad reckoned that he must have begged the dog off someone who'd otherwise have had it destroyed.

The dog began as a secret, which sounds just about impossible, with Mrs Macy around. But every day Mr Macy used to take his dinner and eat it in his tool-shed, which opened on the side furthest from the house. That must have been his temptation; but none of us knew he'd fallen into it, until one summer evening we heard a most awful screeching from the Macys' house.

"That's old Ma Macy screaming," said Dad, spreading his bread and butter.

"Oh, dear!" said Mum, jumping up and then sitting down again. "Poor old Mr Macy!" But Mum was afraid of Mrs Macy. "Run upstairs, boy, and see if you can see what's going on."

So I did. I was just in time for the excitement, for, as I leaned out of the window, the Macys' back door flew open. Mr Macy came out first, with his head down and his arms sort of curved above it; and Mrs Macy came out close behind him, aiming at his head with a light broom—but aiming quite hard. She was screeching words, although it was difficult to pick out any of them. But some words came again and again, and I began to follow: Mr Macy had brought hairs with him into the house—short, curly, yellowish hairs, and he'd left those hairs all over the upholstery, and they must have come from a cat or a dog or a hamster or I don't know what, and so on and so on. Whatever the creature was, he'd been keeping it in the tool-shed, and turn it out he was going to, this very minute.

As usual, Mrs Macy was right about what Mr Macy was going to do.

He opened the shed-door and out ambled a dog—a big, yellowy-white old dog, looking a bit like a sheep, somehow, and about as quick-witted. As though it didn't notice what a tantrum Mrs Macy was in, it blundered gently towards her, and she lifted her broom high, and Mr Macy covered his eyes; and then Mrs Macy let out a real scream—a plain shriek—and dropped the broom and shot indoors and slammed the door after her.

The dog seemed puzzled, naturally; and so was I. It lumbered around towards Mr Macy, and then I saw its head properly, and that it had the most extraordinary eyes—like headlamps, somehow. I don't mean as big as headlamps, of course, but with a kind of whitish glare to them. Then I realised that the poor old thing must be blind.

The dog had raised its nose inquiringly towards Mr Macy, and Mr Macy had taken one timid, hopeful step towards the dog, when one of the sash-windows of the house went up and Mrs Macy leaned out. She'd recovered from her panic, and she gave Mr Macy his orders. He was to take that disgusting animal and turn it out into the road, where he must have found it in the first place.

I knew that old Macy would be too dead scared to do anything else but what his wife told him.

I went down again to where the others were having tea.

"Well?" said Mum.

I told them, and I told them what Mrs Macy was making Mr Macy do to the blind dog. "And if it's turned out like that on the road, it'll be killed by the first car that comes along."

There was a pause, when even Nora seemed to be thinking; but I could see from their faces what they were thinking.

Dad said at last: "That's bad. But we've four people in this little house, and a dog already, and a cat and two birds. There's no room for anything else."

"But it'll be killed."

"No," said Dad. "Not if you go at once, before any car comes, and take that dog down to the village, to the police-station. Tell them it's a stray."

"But what'll they do with it?"

Dad looked as though he wished I hadn't asked that, but he said: "Nothing, I expect. Well, they might hand it over to the Cruelty to Animals people."

"And what'll *they* do with it?"

Dad was rattled. "They do what they think best for animals—I should have thought they'd have taught you that at school. For goodness sake, boy!"

Dad wasn't going to say any more, nor Mum, who'd been listening with her lips pursed up. But everyone knew that the most likely thing was that an old, blind, ownerless dog would be destroyed.

But anything would be better than being run over and killed by a car just as you were sauntering along in the evening sunlight; so I started out of the house after the dog.

There he was, sauntering along, just as I'd imagined him. No sign of Mr Macy, of course: he'd have been called back indoors by his wife.

As I ran to catch up with the dog, I saw Dirty Dick coming home, and nearer the dog than I was. He was pushing his handcart, loaded with the usual bits of wood and other junk. He saw the dog coming and stopped, and waited; the dog came on hesitantly towards him.

"I'm coming for him," I called.

"Ah," said Dirty Dick. "Yours?" He held out his hand towards the dog—the hand that my mother always said she could only bear to take hold of if the owner had to be pulled from certain death in a quicksand. Anyway, the dog couldn't see the colour of it, and it positively seemed to like the smell; it came on.

"No," I said. "Macys were keeping it, but Mrs Macy turned it out. I'm going to take it down to the police as a stray. What do you think they'll do with it?"

Dirty Dick never said much; this time he didn't answer. He just bent down to get his arm round the dog and in a second he'd hoisted him up on top of all the stuff in the cart. Then he picked up the handles and started off again.

So the Macys saw the blind dog come back to the row of cottages in state, as you might say, sitting on top of half a broken lavatory-seat on the very pinnacle of Dirty Dick's latest load of junk.

Dirty Dick took good care of his animals, and he took good care of this dog he adopted. It always looked well-fed and well-brushed. Sometimes he'd take it out with him, on the end of a long string; mostly he'd leave it comfortably at home. When it lay out in the back-garden, old Mr Macy used to look at it longingly over the fence. Once or twice I saw him poke his fingers through, towards what had once been *his* dog. But that had been for only a very short, dark time in the shed; and the old dog never moved towards the fingers. Then "Macy!" his terrible old wife would call from the house, and he'd have to go.

Then suddenly we heard that Dirty Dick had been robbed—old Macy came round specially to tell us. "An old sock stuffed with pound notes, that he kept up the bedroom chimney. Gone. Hasn't he *told* you?"

"No," said Mum, "but we don't have a lot to do with

him." She might have added that we didn't have a lot to do with the Macys either—I think this was the first time I'd ever seen one step over our threshold in a neighbourly way.

"You're thick with him sometimes," said old Macy, turning on me. "Hasn't he told *you* all about it?"

"Me?" I said. "No."

"Mind you, the whole thing's not to be wondered at," said the old man. "Front and back doors never locked, and money kept in the house. That's a terrible temptation to anyone with a weakness that way. A temptation that shouldn't have been put."

"I daresay," said Mum. "It's a shame, all the same. His savings."

"Perhaps the police'll be able to get it back for him," I said. "There'll be clues."

The old man jumped—a nervous sort of jump. "Clues? You think the police will find clues? I never thought of that. No, I did not. But has he gone to the police, anyway, I wonder. That's what I wonder. That's what I'm asking you." He paused, and I realised that he meant me again. "You're thick with him, boy. Has he gone to the police? That's what I want to know . . ."

His mouth seemed to have filled with saliva, so that he had to stop to swallow, and couldn't say more. He was in a state, all right.

At that moment Dad walked in from work and wasn't best pleased to find that visitor instead of his tea waiting; and Mr Macy went.

Dad listened to the story over tea, and across the fence that evening he spoke to Dirty Dick and said he was sorry to hear about the money.

"Who told you?" asked Dirty Dick.

Dad said that old Macy had told us. Dirty Dick just nodded; he didn't seem interested in talking about it any more. Over that weekend no police came to the row, and you might have thought that old Macy had invented the whole thing, except that Dirty Dick had not contradicted him.

On Monday I was rushing off to school when I saw Mr Macy in their front garden, standing just between a big laurel bush and the fence. He looked straight at me and said "Good morning" in a kind of whisper. I don't know which was odder—the whisper, or his wishing me good morning. I answered in rather a shout, because I was late and hurrying past. His mouth had opened as though he meant to say more, but then it shut, as though he'd changed his mind. That was all, that morning.

The next morning he was in just the same spot again, and hailed me in the same way; and this time I was early, so I stopped.

He was looking shiftily about him, as though someone might be spying on us; but at least his wife couldn't be doing that, because the laurel bush was between him and their front windows. There was a tiny pile of yellow froth at one corner of his mouth, as though he'd been chewing his words over in advance. The sight of the froth made me want not to stay; but then the way he looked at me made me feel that I had to. No, it just made me; I had to.

"Look what's turned up in our back-garden," he said, in the same whispering voice. And he held up a sock so dirty—partly with soot—and so smelly that it could only have been Dirty Dick's. It was stuffed full of something—pound notes, in fact. Old Macy's story of the robbery had been true in every detail.

I gaped at him.

"It's all to go back," said Mr Macy. "Back exactly to where it came from." And then, as though I'd suggested the obvious—that he should hand the sock back to Dirty Dick himself with the same explanation just given to me: "No, no. It must go back as though it had never been—never been taken away." He couldn't use the word "stolen". "Mustn't have the police poking round us. Mrs Macy wouldn't like it." His face twitched at his own mention of her; he leaned forward. "You must put it back, boy. Put it back for me and keep your mouth shut. Go on. Yes."

He must have been half out of his mind to think that I should do it, especially as I still didn't twig why. But as I stared at his twitching face I suddenly did understand. I mean, that old Macy had taken the sock, out of spite, and then lost his nerve.

He must have been half out of his mind to think that I would do that for him; and yet I did it. I took the sock and put it inside my jacket and turned back to Dirty Dick's cottage. I walked boldly up to the front door and knocked, and of course there was no answer. I knew he was already out with the cart.

There wasn't a sign of anyone looking, either from our house or the Macys'. (Mr Macy had already disappeared.) I tried the door and it opened, as I knew it would. I stepped inside and closed it behind me.

I'd never been inside before. The house was dirty, I suppose, and smelt a bit, but not really badly. It smelt of Dirty Dick and hens and rabbits—although it was untrue that he kept either hens or rabbits indoors, as Mrs Macy said. It smelt of dog, too, of course.

Opening straight off the living-room, where I stood, was the twisty, dark little stairway—exactly as in our cottage next door.

I went up.

The first room upstairs was full of junk. A narrow passageway had been kept clear to the second room, which opened off the first one. This was Dirty Dick's bedroom, with the bed unmade, as it probably was for weeks on end.

There was the fire-place, too, with a good deal of soot which had recently been brought down from the chimney. You couldn't miss seeing that—Dirty Dick couldn't have missed it, at the time. Yet he'd done nothing about his theft. In fact, I realised now that he'd probably said nothing either. The only person who'd let the cat out of the bag was poor old Macy himself.

I'd been working this out as I looked at the fire-place, standing quite still. Round me the house was silent. The only sound came from outside, where I could see a hen perched on the bumper of the old car in the back-garden, clucking for an egg newly laid. But when she stopped, there came another, tiny sound that terrified me: the click of a front-gate opening. Feet were clumping up to the front door . . .

I stuffed the sock up the chimney again, any old how, and was out of that bedroom in seconds; but on the threshold of the junk-room I stopped, fixed by the headlamp glare of the old blind dog. He must have been there all the time, lying under a three-legged washstand, on a heap of rags. All the time he would have been watching me, if he'd had his eyesight. He didn't move.

Meanwhile the front door had opened and the footsteps had clumped inside, and stopped. There was a long pause, while I stared at the dog, who stared at me; and down below Dirty Dick listened and waited—he must have heard my movement just before.

At last: "Well," he called, "why don't you come down?"

There was nothing else to do but go. Down that dark, twisty stair, knowing that Dirty Dick was waiting for me at the bottom. He was a big man, and strong. He heaved his junk about like nobody's business.

But when I got down, he wasn't by the foot of the stairs; he was standing by the open door, looking out, with his back to me. He hadn't been surprised to hear someone upstairs in his house, uninvited; but when he turned round from the doorway, I could see that he hadn't expected to see *me*. He'd expected someone else —old Macy, I suppose.

I wanted to explain that I'd only put the sock back— there was soot all over my hands, plain to be seen, of course—and that I'd had nothing to do with taking it in the first place. But he'd drawn his thick brows together as he looked at me, and he jerked his head towards the open door. I was frightened, and I went past him without saying anything. I was late for school now, anyway, and I ran.

I didn't see Dirty Dick again.

Later that morning Mum chose to give him a talking to, over the back fence, about locking his doors against pilferers in future. She says he didn't say he would, he didn't say he wouldn't; and he didn't say anything about anything having been stolen, or returned.

Soon after that, Mum saw him go out with the hand-cart with all his rabbits in a hutch, and he came back later without them. He did the same with his hens. We heard later that he'd given them away in the village; he hadn't even bothered to try to sell them.

Then he went round to Mum, wheeling the tricycle. He said he'd decided not to use it any more, and I could have it. He didn't leave any message for me.

Later still, Mum saw him set off for the third time that day with his hand-cart: not piled very high even, but with the old dog sitting on top. And that was the last that anyone saw of him.

He must have taken very little money with him: they found the sooty sock, still nearly full, by the rent-book on the mantelpiece. There was plenty to pay the rent due and to pay for cleaning up the house and the garden for the next tenant. He must have been fed up with being a householder, Dad said—and with having neighbours. He just wanted to turn tramp, and he did.

It was soon after he'd gone that I said to Mum that I envied him, and she blew me up, and went on and on about soap and water and fecklessness. All the same, I did envy him. I didn't even have the fun with his tricycle that he'd had. I never rode it, although I wanted to, because I was afraid that people I knew would laugh at me.

In the Middle of the Night

In the middle of the night a fly woke Charlie. At first he lay listening, half-asleep, while it swooped about the room. Sometimes it was far; sometimes it was near—that was what had woken him; and occasionally it was very near indeed. It was very, very near when the buzzing stopped: the fly had alighted on his face. He jerked his head up; the fly buzzed off. Now he was really awake.

The fly buzzed widely about the room, but it was thinking of Charlie all the time. It swooped nearer and nearer. Nearer . . .

Charlie pulled his head down under the bedclothes.

All of him under the bedclothes, he was completely protected; but he could hear nothing except his heartbeats and his breathing. He was overwhelmed by the smell of warm bedding, warm pyjamas, warm himself. He was going to suffocate. So he rose suddenly up out of the bedclothes; and the fly was waiting for him. It dashed at him. He beat at it with his hands. At the same time he appealed to his younger brother, Wilson, in the next bed: "Wilson, there's a fly!"

Wilson, unstirring, slept on.

Now Charlie and the fly were pitting their wits against each other: Charlie pouncing on the air where he thought the fly must be; the fly sliding under his guard towards his face. Again and again the fly reached Charlie; again and again, almost simultaneously, Charlie dislodged him. Once he hit the fly—or, at least, hit where the fly had been a second before, on the side of his head; the blow was so hard that his head sang with it afterwards.

Then suddenly the fight was over; no more buzzing. His blows—or rather, one of them—must have told.

He laid his head back on the pillow, thinking of going to sleep again. But he was also thinking of the fly, and now he noticed a tickling in the ear he turned to the pillow.

It must be—it *was*—the fly.

He rose in such panic that the waking of Wilson really seemed to him a possible thing, and useful. He shook him repeatedly: "Wilson—Wilson, I tell you, there's a fly in my ear!"

Wilson groaned, turned over very slowly like a seal in water, and slept on.

The tickling in Charlie's ear continued. He could just imagine the fly struggling in some passage-way too narrow for its wing-span. He longed to put his finger into his ear and rattle it round, like a stick in a rabbit-hole; but he was afraid of driving the fly deeper into his ear.

Wilson slept on.

Charlie stood in the middle of the bedroom floor, quivering and trying to think. He needed to see down his ear, or to get someone else to see down it. Wilson wouldn't do; perhaps Margaret would.

Margaret's room was next door. Charlie turned on the light as he entered: Margaret's bed was empty. He was startled, and then thought that she must have gone to the lavatory. But there was no light from there. He listened carefully: there was no sound from anywhere, except for the usual snuffling moans from the hall, where Floss slept and dreamt of dog-biscuits. The empty bed was mystifying; but Charlie had his ear to worry about. It sounded as if there were a pigeon inside it now.

Wilson asleep; Margaret vanished; that left Alison. But Alison was bossy, just because she was the eldest; and, anyway, she would probably only wake Mum. He might as well wake Mum himself.

Down the passage and through the door always left ajar. "Mum," he said. She woke, or at least half-woke, at once: "Who is it? Who? Who? What's the matter? What?—"

"I've a fly in my ear."

"You can't have."

"It flew in."

She switched on the bedside light, and, as she did so, Dad plunged beneath the bedclothes with an exclamation and lay still again.

Charlie knelt at his mother's side of the bed and she looked into his ear. "There's nothing."

"Something crackles."

"It's wax in your ear."

"It tickles."

"There's no fly there. Go back to bed and stop imagining things."

His father's arm came up from below the bedclothes. The hand waved about, settled on the bedside light and clicked it out. There was an upheaval of bedclothes and a comfortable grunt.

"Goodnight," said Mum from the darkness. She was already allowing herself to sink back into sleep again.

"Goodnight," Charlie said sadly. Then an idea occurred to him. He repeated his goodnight loudly and added some coughing, to cover the fact that he was closing the bedroom door behind him—the door that Mum kept open so that she could listen for her children. They had outgrown all that kind of attention, except possibly for Wilson. Charlie had shut the door against Mum's hearing because he intended to slip downstairs for a drink of water—well, for a drink and perhaps a snack. That fly-business had woken him up and also weakened him: he needed something.

He crept downstairs, trusting to Floss's good sense not to make a row. He turned the foot of the staircase towards the kitchen, and there had not been the faintest whimper from her, far less a bark. He was passing the dog-basket when he had the most unnerving sensation of something being wrong there—something unusual, at least. He could not have said whether he had heard something or smelt something—he could certainly have seen nothing in the blackness: perhaps some extra sense warned him.

"Floss?" he whispered, and there was the usual little scrabble and snuffle. He held out his fingers low down for Floss to lick. As she did not do so at once, he moved them towards her, met some obstruction—

"Don't poke your fingers in my eye!" a voice said, very low-toned and cross. Charlie's first, confused thought was that Floss had spoken: the voice was familiar—but then a voice from Floss should *not* be familiar; it should be strangely new to him—

He took an uncertain little step towards the voice, tripped over the obstruction, which was quite wrong in shape and size to be Floss, and sat down. Two things now happened. Floss, apparently having climbed over the obstruction, reached his lap and began to lick his face. At the same time a human hand fumbled over his face, among the slappings of Floss's tongue, and settled over his mouth. "Don't make a row! Keep quiet!" said the same voice. Charlie's mind cleared: he knew, although without understanding, that he was sitting on the floor in the dark with Floss on his knee and Margaret beside him.

Her hand came off his mouth.

"What are you doing here, anyway, Charlie?"

"I like that! What about you? There was a fly in my ear."

"Go on!"

"There was."

"Why does that make you come downstairs?"

"I wanted a drink of water."

"There's water in the bathroom."

"Well, I'm a bit hungry."

"If Mum catches you . . ."

"Look here," Charlie said, "you tell me what you're doing down here."

Margaret sighed. "Just sitting with Floss."

"You can't come down and just sit with Floss in the middle of the night."

"Yes, I can. I keep her company. Only at weekends, of course. No one seemed to realise what it was like for her when those puppies went. She just couldn't get to sleep for loneliness."

"But the last puppy went weeks ago. You haven't been keeping Floss company every Saturday night since then."

"Why not?"

Charlie gave up. "I'm going to get my food and drink," he said. He went into the kitchen, followed by Margaret, followed by Floss.

They all had a quick drink of water. Then Charlie and Margaret looked into the larder: the remains of a joint; a very large quantity of mashed potato; most of a loaf; eggs; butter; cheese . . .

"I suppose it'll have to be just bread and butter and a bit of cheese," said Charlie. "Else Mum might notice."

"Something hot," said Margaret. "I'm cold from sitting in the hall comforting Floss. I need hot cocoa, I think." She poured some milk into a saucepan and put it on the hot plate. Then she began a search for the tin of cocoa. Charlie, standing by the cooker, was already absorbed in the making of a rough cheese sandwich.

The milk in the pan began to steam. Given time, it rose in the saucepan, peered over the top, and boiled over on to the hot plate, where it sizzled loudly. Margaret rushed back and pulled the saucepan to one side. "Well, really, Charlie! Now there's that awful smell! It'll still be here in the morning, too."

"Set the fan going," Charlie suggested.

The fan drew the smell from the cooker up and away through a pipe to the outside. It also made a loud roaring noise. Not loud enough to reach their parents, who slept on the other side of the house—that was all that Charlie and Margaret thought of.

Alison's bedroom, however, was immediately above the kitchen. Charlie was eating his bread and cheese, Margaret was drinking her cocoa, when the kitchen door opened and there stood Alison. Only Floss was pleased to see her.

"Well!" she said.

Charlie muttered something about a fly in his ear, but Margaret said nothing. Alison had caught them red-handed. She would call Mum downstairs, that was obvious. There would be an awful row.

Alison stood there. She liked commanding a situation.

Then, instead of taking a step backwards to call up the stairs to Mum, she took a step forward into the kitchen. "What are you having, anyway?" she asked. She glanced with scorn at Charlie's poor piece of bread and cheese and at Margaret's cocoa. She moved over to the larder, flung open the door, and looked searchingly inside. In such a way must Napoleon have viewed a battlefield before the victory.

Her gaze fell upon the bowl of mashed potato. "I shall make potato-cakes," said Alison.

They watched while she brought the mashed potato to the kitchen table. She switched on the oven, fetched her other ingredients, and began mixing.

"Mum'll notice if you take much of that potato," said Margaret.

But Alison thought big. "She may notice if some potato is missing," she agreed. "But if there's none at all, and if the bowl it was in is washed and dried and stacked away with the others, then she's going to think she must have made a mistake. There just can never have been any mashed potato."

Alison rolled out her mixture and cut it into cakes; then she set the cakes on a baking-tin and put it in the oven.

Now she did the washing up. Throughout the time they were in the kitchen, Alison washed up and put away as she went along. She wanted no one's help. She was very methodical, and she did everything herself to be sure that nothing was left undone. In the morning there must be no trace left of the cooking in the middle of the night.

"And now," said Alison, "I think we should fetch Wilson."

The other two were aghast at the idea; but Alison was firm in her reasons. "It's better if we're all in this together, Wilson as well. Then, if the worst comes to the worst, it won't be just us three caught out, with Wilson hanging on to Mum's apron-strings, smiling innocence. We'll all be for it together; and Mum'll be softer with us if we've got Wilson."

They saw that, at once. But Margaret still objected: "Wilson will tell. He just always tells everything. He can't help it."

Alison said, "He always tells everything. Right: we'll give him something *to* tell, and then see if Mum believes him. We'll do an entertainment for him. Get an umbrella from the hall and Wilson's sou'-wester and a blanket or a rug or something. Go on."

They would not obey Alison's orders until they had heard her plan; then they did. They fetched the umbrella and the hat, and lastly they fetched Wilson, still sound asleep, slung between the two of them in his eiderdown. They propped him in a chair at the kitchen table, where he still slept.

By now the potato-cakes were done. Alison took them out of the oven and set them on the table before Wilson. She buttered them, handing them in turn to Charlie and Margaret and helping herself. One was set aside to cool for Floss.

The smell of fresh-cooked, buttery potato-cake woke Wilson, as was to be expected. First his nose sipped the air, then his eyes opened, his gaze settled on the potato-cakes.

"Like one?" Alison asked.

Wilson opened his mouth wide and Alison put a potato-cake inside, whole.

"They're paradise-cakes," Alison said.

"Potato-cakes?" said Wilson, recognising the taste.

"No, paradise-cakes, Wilson," and then, stepping aside, she gave him a clear view of Charlie's and Margaret's entertainment, with the umbrella and the sou'wester hat and his eiderdown. "Look, Wilson, look."

Wilson watched with wide-open eyes, and into his wide-open mouth Alison put, one by one, the potato-cakes that were his share.

But, as they had foreseen, Wilson did not stay awake for very long. When there were no more potato-cakes, he yawned, drowsed, and suddenly was deeply asleep. Charlie and Margaret put him back into his eiderdown and took him upstairs to bed again. They came down to return the umbrella and the sou'wester to their proper places, and to see Floss back into her basket. Alison, last out of the kitchen, made sure that everything was in its place.

The next morning Mum was down first. On Sunday she always cooked a proper breakfast for anyone there in time. Dad was always there in time; but this morning Mum was still looking for a bowl of mashed potato when he appeared.

"I can't think where it's gone," she said. "I can't think."

"I'll have the bacon and eggs without the potato," said Dad; and he did. While he ate, Mum went back to searching.

Wilson came down, and was sent upstairs again to put on a dressing-gown. On his return he said that Charlie was still asleep and there was no sound from the girls' rooms either. He said he thought they were tired out. He went on talking while he ate his breakfast. Dad was reading the paper and Mum had gone back to poking about in the larder for the bowl of mashed potato, but Wilson liked talking even if no one would listen. When

Mum came out of the larder for a moment, still without her potato, Wilson was saying: ". . . and Charlie sat in an umbrella-boat on an eiderdown-sea, and Margaret pretended to be a sea-serpent, and Alison gave us paradise-cakes to eat. Floss had one too, but it was too hot for her. What are paradise-cakes? Dad, what's a paradise-cake?"

"Don't know," said Dad, reading.

"Mum, what's a paradise-cake?"

"Oh, Wilson, don't bother so when I'm looking for something . . . When did you eat this cake, anyway?"

"I told you. Charlie sat in his umbrella-boat on an eiderdown-sea and Margaret was a sea-serpent and Alison—"

"Wilson," said his mother, "you've been dreaming."

"No, really—really!" Wilson cried.

But his mother paid no further attention. "I give up," she said. "That mashed potato: it must have been last weekend . . ." She went out of the kitchen to call the others: "Charlie! Margaret! Alison!"

Wilson, in the kitchen, said to his father, "I wasn't dreaming. And Charlie said there was a fly in his ear."

Dad had been quarter-listening; now he put down his paper. "What?"

"Charlie had a fly in his ear."

Dad stared at Wilson. "And what did you say that Alison fed you with?"

"Paradise-cakes. She'd just made them, I think, in the middle of the night."

"What were they like?"

"Lovely. Hot, with butter. Lovely."

"But were they—well, could they have had any mashed potato in them, for instance?"

In the hall Mum was finishing her calling: "Charlie! Margaret! Alison! I warn you now!"

"I don't know about that," Wilson said. "They were paradise-cakes. They tasted a bit like the potato-cakes Mum makes, but Alison said they weren't. She specially said they were paradise-cakes."

Dad nodded. "You've finished your breakfast. Go up and get dressed, and you can take this"—he took a coin from his pocket—"straight off to the sweet-shop. Go on."

Mum met Wilson at the kitchen door: "Where's he off to in such a hurry?"

"I gave him something to buy sweets with," said Dad. "I wanted a quiet breakfast. He talks too much."

The Tree in the Meadow

There were buildings on three sides of Miss Mortlock's meadow; on the fourth, the river. In the middle of the meadow stood the elm. There were other trees in the meadow: sycamore, ash, horse-chestnut. The elm was giant among them. It had always stood there. Nobody remembered its being younger than it was; nobody remembered it less than its present immense height. Nobody really thought about it any more. They saw it, simply.

Then one day a branch fell from the elm-tree. It seemed just to tear itself off from the main body of the tree. There was nothing to show why, except for a discoloration of wood at the torn end.

At its thickest, the branch that fell was almost the thickness of a man's body.

The fall caused some surprise in the houses over-looking the meadow; but nobody thought more about the incident until—no, not the next year, but the year after that—another branch dropped. The meadow had been cut for hay, and the Scarr children had been making hay-houses. They had just gone in to tea when the branch—quite as big as the previous one—fell. It fell where they had been playing, smashing and scatter-ing their hay-houses. Mrs Scarr was very much upset at what might have happened—at what *would* have happened if the children had still been playing there. Mr Scarr agreed that the possibilities were upsetting; and he now pointed out that the rooks no longer nested in the elm. *They* knew. Some day—one day before too long—the whole tree would fall. It would fall without warning, and the damage could only be guessed at. The elm might fall on Miss Mortlock's house; it might fall on the Scarrs' house; it might fall on the buildings the other side—old Mortlock stables and outhouses, no great loss if they were smashed, but a mess. Or—if everyone had great good luck—the elm might fall harmlessly away from all buildings, across the meadow towards the river.

Miss Mortlock was now told that she ought to have the elm taken down.

Miss Mortlock said that the elm had been there long before she was born and she hoped and expected that it would be there after she was dead. She wanted no advice on the subject.

Another branch fell from the elm tree, partly squashing a farm-trailer. The farmer whose trailer it was had been renting the meadow from Miss Mortlock for his cows. He tried to make Miss Mortlock pay the value of the trailer. Miss Mortlock replied that he had left his trailer in a particularly foolish place. She could not be held responsible. Everyone knew what elm-trees were like, especially when they were getting old and rotten. No doubt he had heard of previous branches falling.

Mr Scarr had another conversation with Miss Mortlock about having the elm-tree felled. She said that these tree-surgeons, as they called themselves, used fancy equipment so that they could charge fancy prices. She could not afford them.

Mr Scarr said that he knew two handymen, pals, with a cross-cut saw, axe, wedges, and good rope. They could fell any tree to within six inches of where it should go. Miss Mortlock was surprised and delighted to hear that there was anybody who would come and do anything well, nowadays. Through Mr Scarr, a bargain was struck between Miss Mortlock and the handymen.

Mr Scarr told his family about the arrangement over tea. Mrs Scarr sighed with relief and thought no more of it—until later. The little girls were too young to understand. Only Ricky was interested. He said: "What will happen to the tree?"

His father stared at him. "It'll be felled. Didn't you hear me?"

"I mean, what will happen to the tree after that?" He had once seen a lorry passing through the village carrying an enormous tree-trunk, lopped of all its branches, chained down.

"It won't be a tree when it's felled," said Mr Scarr.

"Timber. Poor timber, in this case. Not sound enough even for coffins. Not worth cartage."

That night Ricky looked out of his bedroom window over the meadow to the elm. It stood, a tree. It was leafless, at this time of year, and the outer twigs on one side made what you could think of as the shape of a woman's head with fluffed-out hair, face bent downwards. He had seen that woman from his window ever since he could remember.

He tried to imagine the elm-tree cut down; not there. He tried to imagine space where the trunk and branches and twigs were—the whole great shape missing from the meadow. He tried to imagine looking right across the meadow without the interruption of the tree; looking across emptiness to the stables on the other side. He could not.

The next day, on his way to school, Ricky called as usual for Willy Jim, his best friend, who lived at the top of the lane. They went on together, and Ricky said: "Our elm's being cut down."

"So what?" said Willy Jim, preoccupied. He was still Ricky's best friend, perhaps, but he was also in with a new gang at school. Ricky wanted to get into the same gang. He meant to try, anyway.

In the playground, later, Ricky said to Bones Jones, who was leader of the gang: "Our elm-tree's going to be cut down. It's hundreds of years old; it's hundreds of feet high."

"Didn't know you owned an elm."

"Well, the elm in our meadow."

"Didn't know you owned a meadow."

"Oh, well—Miss Mortlock's meadow. She lets us

play in it. Shall I let you know when they're going to cut the elm down?"

"If you like."

Later still that day, Toffy, a friend of Bones Jones, spoke to Ricky, which he did not often bother to do. He said: "I hope they cut that tree down after school, or on a Saturday. Otherwise we'll miss it." So Bones Jones had told Toffy and the others.

And when they were all going home from school, Bones Jones called to Ricky: "Don't forget to find out about what you said. Might be worth watching."

Surprisingly, Ricky had difficulty in getting his piece of information. His father was vague, even mysterious, about when exactly the elm would be felled. He glanced several times at his wife, during Ricky's questioning. She listened in silence, grim.

So Ricky first knew when, looking out of his window just after getting up one morning, he saw a truck in the meadow, with a ladder on its roof, and two men unloading gear that would clearly turn out to be saw, axe, wedges and rope.

At breakfast his mother said to his father: "If they start now, they'll have finished before the afternoon, won't they?"

"Likely," said Mr Scarr.

"So that wicked tree'll be safely down by the time you get home from school," his mother said to Ricky. Ricky scowled.

But there was still one chance, and Ricky thought it worth taking.

On the way to school he told Willy Jim; in the playground he told Bones Jones, Toffy, and the two others who made up the gang. "They're starting on the elm this morning. If we go to the meadow between the end of school-dinner and the beginning of afternoon school, we might be lucky. We might see the fall."

The older children were allowed out of school after dinner to go to the sweetshop. The six boys would need only to turn right towards the lane, instead of left towards the sweetshop, when they set off at the permitted time. They would have about twenty minutes.

So, between one o'clock and a quarter past, the whole gang, including Ricky, were tearing down the lane to Miss Mortlock's meadow. They halted at the meadow-gate, surprised; Ricky himself felt abashed. The truck and handymen had gone, although wheel-tracks showed they had been there. The elm still stood. At first sight, nothing had happened or was going to happen.

Then they noticed something about the base of the tree. They climbed the gate and went over. A wide gash had been chopped out of the trunk on the side towards the river. On the opposite side, at the same level, the tree had been sawn almost half through.

Ricky, remembering his father's talk, said: "They'll drive the wedges in there, where they've sawn. When the time comes."

It now occurred to them to wonder where *they* were —the handymen, the tree-fellers. Toffy recollected having noticed a truck going up the village in the direction of The Peacock. The handymen, having done most of the hard work, had probably broken for a pint at The Peacock. After that, they would come back and finish the job.

Meanwhile, the boys had the elm-tree to themselves.

They were examining the saw-cut, all except for Ricky. He had gone round almost to the other side of the tree. Clasping the trunk with his arms, he pressed his body close against it, tipped his head back, and let his gaze go mountaineering up into the tree—up—up—

Then he saw it, and wondered that he had not noticed it at once: the rope. It had been secured to the main part of the tree as near to the top as possible. Its length fell straight through the branches to the ground, passing near the finger-tips of one of his hands. It reached the ground, where more of it—much more of it—lay at the foot of the tree, coiled round and ready for use.

"Look!" said Ricky.

The others came round the tree and gathered where the rope fell, staring at it; then staring up into the tree, to where the end was fastened; then staring across the meadow towards the river.

Bones Jones said: "We could take the rope out over the meadow. That wouldn't do any harm."

Toffy said: "Not with us not pulling on it."

Willy Jim said: "And not with the wedges not in."

Ricky said nothing.

All the same, they were very careful to take the loose end of the rope over the meadow towards the river, keeping as far as possible from the buildings on either side. They walked backwards towards the river, dragging the rope. At first, it dragged slackly through the rough grass of the meadow. Then, as they walked with it, it began to lift a little from the ground. They still walked, and the deep, floppy curve of it began to grow shallower and shallower—nearer and nearer to a straight line running from the boys to the top of the elm-tree. They pulled it almost taut, and paused.

Toffy said: "This is about where they'll stand."

Bones Jones said: "And pull."

They arranged themselves in what seemed to them a correct order along the rope, with the heaviest at the end. That was Bones Jones himself. Then came Toffy, then the other two and Willy Jim, and lastly Ricky, the lightest of all, nearest to the tree.

"And pull," repeated Bones Jones; and they pulled very gently, slightly tautening the rope so that it ran from their hands in that straight, straight line to the top of the elm-tree.

The cows that were grazing in the meadow had moved off slowly but intently to the furthest distance, against the old stables.

"Only the pulling would have to be in time," said Bones Jones. "You know: one, two, three, *pull*, rest; one, two, three, *pull*, rest. Feeling the sway of the tree, once it started swaying. Before it falls."

Miss Mortlock's dog, a King Charles spaniel, appeared at the gate into the meadow and stared at the boys. He was old and he didn't like boys, but this was his meadow. He came through the gate and towards what was going on. He stood between the tree and the boys, but some way off, watching. After a while he sat down, with the regretful slowness of someone who has forgotten to bring his shooting-stick.

They were getting the rhythm now, slow but strong: "One, two, three, and *pull*, rest; one, two, three, and *pull*, rest . . ." They were chanting in perfect time under their breaths; in perfect time they were pulling, gently, well.

Mrs Scarr, looking up from her sink and out through the kitchen-window, might have seen them; but the sweetbriar hedge was in the way.

Miss Mortlock did see them, from an upper window. She had gone up to take an after-lunch nap on her bed, and was about to draw the curtains. She looked out. Her eyesight was not good nowadays, but she knew boys when she saw them, and she knew at once what they must be doing. She saw that the elm-tree was beginning a slow, graceful waving of its topmost branches. Very slightly: this-a-way; that-a-way. Only each time it swayed, the sway was more this-a-way, towards the river, than that-a-way, towards the house.

This-a-way; that-a-way . . .

Miss Mortlock knocked on the window-pane with her knuckles, but the boys could not hear the distant tapping. She called, but they could not hear her old woman's voice. She tried to push open the sash-window, but that window had not been opened at the bottom for twenty years, and it was not going to be rushed now.

This-a-way; that-a-way; *this*-a-way—that-a-way—

"*Pull* . . ." the boys chanted, ". . . and *pull* . . . and *pull* . . ."

They did not hear the sound of the truck driving up to the meadow-gate again. The two handymen saw. They began to shout even before they were out of the truck: "No!"

The cows lifted their heads to look towards the elm.

"Oh, no!" cried Miss Mortlock from the wrong side of the window-glass.

The King Charles spaniel stood up and began to growl.

". . . and *pull* . . . and *pull* . . ."

"No!" whispered Ricky to himself.

For the rope they pulled on was no longer taut, even when they pulled it. It came slackly to them. There was a great, unimaginable creak, and then the elm began to lean courteously towards them. They stood staring; and the tree leaned over—over—reaching its tallness to reach them; and they saw what only the birds and the aeroplanes had ever seen before—the very crown of the tree, and it was roaring down towards them—

"NO!" screamed Ricky, who was nearest to it, seeing right into those reaching, topmost branches that only the birds and the aeroplanes saw; and the other boys were yelling and scattering, and Miss Mortlock's sash-window shot up suddenly and she was calling shrilly out of it, and the handymen were vaulting the gate and shouting, and the King Charles spaniel was barking, and the elm-tree that had stood forever was crashing to the ground, and Ricky was running, running, running from it, and then tripped and fell face forwards into the nettles on the river-bank and staggered to his feet to run again, but suddenly there was nothing to run on, and fell again. Into the river this time.

The river was not deep or swift-flowing, but muddy. He wallowed and floundered to the bank and clawed a hold there and stood, thigh deep in water, against the bank, still below visibility from the meadow. He listened. There were the mingled sounds of boys shouting and men shouting and a dog barking. He guessed that the men were chasing the boys, and the dog was getting in the way.

But he didn't stay. He waded along the river, in the shelter of the vegetation on its bank, until he reached the end of the meadow. The boundary of the meadow, on this side, was a sweetbriar hedge that, further up, became the hedge of the Scarrs' garden. He crept out, and crept home.

His face tingled all over and had already swollen—even to the eyelids—with nettle-stings, and he was dripping with river-water and with river-mud that stank. His mother, meeting him at the door, and having—at last; who could miss it now?—realised what had happened in the meadow, dealt with him.

No question of his going back to afternoon-school: he ended up in bed. His mother rattled the curtains together angrily and told him to stay exactly where he was until his dad came home.

When she had gone, he slid out of bed and laid a hand on the curtains to part them. But he did not. There was no sound of voices from the meadow now; and he didn't really want to see. He had thought he wanted to, but he did not. He went back to bed.

His father, home for tea, was far less angry than his mother. He liked the idea of half a dozen schoolboys felling the elm-tree by accident—and Ricky among them. "Didn't think you had it in you," he said to Ricky.

As for punishment, the state of Ricky's face was about as much as was needed, in Mr Scarr's opinion.

And anyway, said Mr Scarr, nobody had expressly

told the boy not to fell the tree. Then Mrs Scarr became very angry with Mr Scarr, as well as with Ricky.

Next day, at school, there was a row, but not too bad. It was over quickly. The rest of the gang had had theirs yesterday. At dinner-time, in the playground, Willy Jim said to Ricky, "You can go around with us, Bones says. We call ourselves Hell Fellows now—Hell Fellers—*fellers*: get it?"

"Oh," said Ricky, "you're one?"

"Yes," said Willy Jim, "and you can be one, too."

So that was all right, of course. Ricky had what he wanted.

Bones Jones decided that, after school, the Hell Fellers would go and look at the tree they had felled. No use going straight from school, however, as Ricky said, because the men would be there, lopping and sawing. So they all went home first to their teas, and then reassembled, singly, carefully casual, at the top of the lane—all except for Ricky, of course, who had his tea and then hung over his front gate, waiting.

When daylight began to fail, the handymen stopped work, packed everything into the truck, shut the meadow-gate, and drove away. They drove out of the top of the lane and, behind them, the boys converged on the entrance to the lane and poured down it. They collected Ricky as they passed his house, then over the meadow-gate and across the meadow to the elm.

Most of its branches had already gone, so that they could clamber up it and along it fairly easily.

Bones Jones, Willy Jim, Ricky—all of them—they clambered, climbed on and jumped off, ran along the trunk. They fought duels along the trunk with lopped-off branches and nearly put each other's eyes out; played a no-holds-barred King of the Castle on the tree-stump; carved their initials in the thickness of the main bark. All they did, they did quietly—with whispers, gasps, grunts, suppressed laughter—for they did not wish to call attention to themselves. There was little fear, otherwise, of their being noticed in the half-light.

Now they gathered together in a line along the trunk. Ricky was in the middle. They linked arms and danced, stamping and singing softly together a song of victory, of Hell Fellers, hell-bent, of victors over the vanquished. The stamping of their feet hardly shook the massive tree-trunk beneath them.

The meadow was almost dark now. Like ghosts they danced along the long ghost of what had once been a tree.

Oblongs of yellow light had appeared in the houses overlooking the meadow. The dancers began to waver. They shivered at the chill of night, and remembered their homes. They stopped dancing. They left the tree-trunk, climbed the gate, went home.

Ricky went home. He was still humming the tune to which they had danced. "You seem pleased with yourself," his mother said grumpily. She had not got over yesterday. Ricky said, "Yes."

When he was going to bed, he looked out of his window, across the meadow. It was quite dark outside, but you could still see which was sky and which was not. He could make out the blackness of the old stables against the sky. There was nothing between him and them. He stared till his eyes watered.

He got into bed thinking of tomorrow and the Hell Fellers at school, pleased. He fell asleep at once, and began dreaming. His own tears woke him. He could not remember his dream, and knew that it had not lasted long, because the same television programme was still going on downstairs.

In the middle of being puzzled at grief, he fell asleep again.

Fresh

The force of water through the river-gates scoured to a deep bottom; then the river shallowed again. People said the pool below the gates was very deep. Deep enough to drown in, anyway.

At the bottom of the pool lived the freshwater mussels. No one had seen them there—most people would not have been particularly interested in them, anyway. But, if you were poking about among the stones in the shallows below the pool, you couldn't help finding mussel-shells occasionally. Sometimes one by itself; sometimes two still hinged together. Grey-blue or green-grey on the outside; on the inside, a faint sheen of mother-of-pearl.

The Webster boys were fishing with their nets in the shallows for minnows, freshwater shrimps—anything that moved—when they found a freshwater mussel that was not just a pair of empty shells.

Dan Webster found it. He said: "Do you want this shell? It's double." While Laurie Webster was saying, "Let's see," Dan was lifting it and had noticed that the two shells were clamped together and that they had unusual weight. "They're not empty shells," he said. "They've something inside. It's alive."

He stooped again to hold the mussel in the palm of his hand so that the river water washed over it. Water-creatures prefer water.

Laurie had splashed over to him. Now he crouched with the river lapping near the tops of his Wellington boots. "A freshwater mussel!" he said. "I've never owned one." He put out fingers to touch it—perhaps to take it—as it lay on the watery palm of Dan's hand. Dan's fingers curled up into a protective wall. "Careful," he said.

Together, as they were now, the Webster boys looked like brothers, but they were cousins. Laurie was the visitor. He lived in London and had an aquarium on his bedroom window-sill, instead of a river almost at his back-door, as Dan had. Dan was older than Laurie; Laurie admired Dan, and Dan was kind to Laurie. They did things together. Dan helped Laurie to find livestock for his aquarium—shrimps, leeches, flatworms, water-snails variously whorled; whatever the turned stone and scooping net might bring them. During a visit by Laurie they would fish often, but—until the last day—without a jam-jar; just for the fun of it. On the last day they took a jam-jar and put their more interesting catches into it, for Laurie's journey back to London.

Now they had found a freshwater mussel on the second day of Laurie's visit. Five more days still to go.

"We can't keep it," said Dan. "Even if we got the jam-jar, it couldn't live in a jam-jar for five days. It would be dead by the time you got it back to the aquarium."

Laurie, who was quite young, looked as if he might cry. "I've never had the chance of a freshwater mussel before."

"Well . . ." said Dan. He made as if to put it down among the stones and mud where he had found it.

"Don't! Don't! It's my freshwater mussel! Don't let it go!"

"And don't shout in my ear!" Dan said crossly. "Who said I was letting it go? I was just trying it out in the river again, to see whether it was safe to leave it there. I don't think the current would carry it away."

He put the mussel down in the shelter of a large, slimy stone. The current, breaking on the stone, flowed past without stirring it. But the mussel began to feel at home again. They could almost see it settling contentedly into the mud. After a while it parted the lips of its shells slightly, and a pastry-like substance crowded out a little way.

"What's it *doing*?" whispered Laurie. But this was not the sort of thing that Dan knew, and Laurie would not find out until he got back to his aquarium-books in London.

Now they saw that they had not merely imagined the

mussel to be settling in. There was less of it visible out of the mud—much less of it.

"It's burying itself. It's escaping," said Laurie. "Don't let it!"

Dan sighed and took the mussel back into the palm of his hand again. The mussel, disappointed, shut up tight.

"We need to keep it in the river," said Dan, "but somewhere where it can't escape."

They looked round. They weren't sure what they were looking for, and at first they certainly weren't finding it.

Still with the mussel in his hand, Dan turned to the banks. They were overhanging, with river-water swirling against them and under them. The roots of trees and bushes made a kind of very irregular lattice fencing through which the water ran continually.

"I wonder . . ." said Dan.

"You couldn't keep it there," Laurie said. "It'd be child's play for a freshwater mussel to escape through the roots."

Dan stared at the roots. "I've a better idea," he said. "I'll stay here with the mussel. You go back to our house—to the larder. You'll find a little white plastic carton with Eileen's slimming cress growing in it." Eileen was Dan's elder sister, whose absorbing interest was her figure. "Empty the cress out on to a plate—I'll square Eileen later. Bring the plastic carton back here."

Laurie never questioned Dan. He set off across the meadows towards the house.

Dan and the freshwater mussel were left alone to wait.

Dan was holding the freshwater mussel as he had done before, stooping down to the river with his hand in the water. It occurred to him to repeat the experiment that Laurie had interrupted. He put the mussel down in the lee of the slimy stone again, and watched. Again, the current left the mussel undisturbed. Again, the mussel began to settle itself into the mud between the stones.

Down—gently down—down . . . The freshwater mussel was now as deep in the mud as when Laurie had called out in fear of losing it; but now Laurie was not there. Dan did not interfere. He simply watched the mussel ease itself down—down . . .

Soon less than a quarter of an inch of mussel shell was showing above the mud. The shell was nearly the same colour as the mud embedding it: Dan could identify it only by keeping his eyes fixed continuously upon its projection. That lessened, until it had almost disappeared.

Entirely disappeared . . .

Still Dan stared. As long as he kept his eyes on the spot where the mussel had disappeared, he could get it again. He had only to dig his fingers into the mud at that exact spot to find it. If he let his eyes stray, the mussel was lost forever; there were so many slimy stones like that one, and mud was everywhere. He must keep his eyes fixed on the spot.

"Dan—Dan—Dan!" Laurie's voice came over the meadows. "I've got it!"

He nearly shifted his stare from the spot by the nondescript stone. It would have been so natural to lift his head in response to the calling voice. He was tempted to do it. But he had to remember that this was Laurie's mussel and it must not be lost: he did remember. He kept his gaze fixed and dug quickly with his fingers and got the mussel again.

There he was standing with the mussel in the palm of his hand, and water and mud dripping from it, when Laurie came in sight. "Is it all right?" he shouted.

"Yes," said Dan.

Laurie climbed down the river-bank into the water with the plastic cress-carton in his hand. Dan looked at it and nodded. "It has holes in the bottom, and we can make some more along the sides with a penknife." He did so, while Laurie held the mussel.

"Now," Dan said, "put the mussel in the carton with some mud and little stones to make it comfortable. That's it. The next thing is to wedge the carton between the roots under the bank at just the right level, so that the water flows through the holes in the carton, without flowing over the whole thing. The mussel will have his flowing river, but he won't be able to escape."

Laurie said, "I wish I could think of things like that."

Dan tried fitting the plastic carton between the roots in several different places, until he found a grip that was just at the right height. Gently, he tested the firmness of the wedging, and it held.

"Oh," said Laurie, "it's just perfect, Dan. Thank you. I shall really get it back to the aquarium, now. My first freshwater mussel. I shall call it—well, what would *you* call it, Dan?"

"Go on," said Dan. "It's your freshwater mussel. You name it."

"I shall call it Fresh, then." Laurie leant forward to

see Fresh, already part-buried in his mud, dim in the shadow of the bank, but absolutely a captive. He stood up again and moved back to admire the arrangement from a distance. Then he realised a weakness. "Oh, it'll never do. The plastic's so white. Anyone might notice it and come over to look, and tip Fresh out."

"We'll hide him then," said Dan. He found an old brick among the stones of the shallows and brought it over to the bank-roots. He up-ended the brick in the water, leaning it in a casual pose against the roots, so that it concealed the white plastic carton altogether.

"There," he said.

Laurie sighed. "Really perfect."

"He should be safe there."

"For five days?"

"I tell you what," said Dan, "we could slip down here every day just to have a check on him. To make sure the level of the water through the carton isn't too high, or hasn't sunk too low."

Laurie nodded. "Every day."

The daily visit to Fresh was a pleasure that Laurie looked forward to. On the third day it poured with rain, but they put on anoraks as well as boots and made their check as usual. On the fourth day they reached the river-bank to find a man fishing on the other side of the pool.

The fisherman was minding his own business and only gave them a sidelong glance as they came to a stop on the bank above Fresh's watery dungeon. (They knew its location exactly by now, even from across the meadow.) The man wasn't interested in them—yet. But if they clambered down into the river and began moving old bricks and poking about behind them, he would take notice. He would ask them what they were up to. When they had gone, he would perhaps come over and have a look for himself. He was wearing waders.

"Not now," Dan said quietly. "Later." And they turned away, as though they had come only to look at the view.

They went back after their tea, but the fisherman was still there. In the meantime, Laurie had worked himself into a desperation. "All that rain yesterday has made the river rise. It'll be washing Fresh out of the carton."

"No," said Dan. "You've just got Fresh on the brain. The river's hardly risen at all. If at all. Fresh is all right."

"Why can't that man go home?"

"He'll go home at dusk, anyway," said Dan.

"That'll be too late for us. I shall be going to bed by then. You know your mum said I must."

"Yes." Dan looked at him thoughtfully. "Would you like *me* to come? I mean, Mum couldn't stop my being out that bit later than you, because I am that bit older."

"Oh, would you—*would* you?" cried Laurie. "Oh, thanks, Dan."

"Oh, don't thank me," said Dan.

Everything went according to plan, except that Dan, getting down to the river just before dark, found the fisherman still there. But he was in the act of packing up. He did not see Dan. He packed up and walked away, whistling sadly to himself. When the whistling had died away, Dan got down into the river and moved the brick and took out the plastic container. It had been at a safe water-level, in spite of the rains, and Fresh was inside, alive and well.

Dan took Fresh out of the carton just to make sure. Then he put him among the stones in the river for the fun of seeing his disappearing act. As he watched, Dan reflected that this was what Fresh would have done if the fisherman *had* spotted the carton and taken him out of it for a good look, and then by mistake dropped him into the water. The fisherman would have lost sight of him, and Fresh would have buried himself. He would have been gone for good; for good, back into the river.

The only signs would have been the brick moved, the plastic container out of place. And Fresh gone. That was all that Dan could have reported to Laurie.

But it had not happened, after all.

Dan picked up Fresh and put him back in the carton and put the carton back and then the brick, and then walked home. He told Laurie, sitting in his pyjamas in front of the TV with his supper, that everything had been all right. He did not say more.

On the fifth day, the day before Laurie's return to London, they went together to the river bank. There was no fisherman. The brick was exactly in place and behind it the plastic carton, with the water flowing through correctly. There was Fresh, safe, sound and apparently not even pining at captivity.

"Tomorrow," said Laurie. "Tomorrow morning we'll bring the jam-jar, ready for me to take him home on the train."

That night was the last of Laurie's visit. He and

Dan shared Dan's bedroom, and tonight they went to bed at the same time, and fell asleep together.

Dan's father was the last person to go to bed at the end of the evening. He bolted the doors and turned out the last lights. That usually did not wake Dan, but tonight it did. Suddenly he was wide awake in the complete darkness, hearing the sound of his parents going to bed in their room, hearing the sound of Laurie's breathing in the next bed, the slow, whispering breath of deep sleep.

The movements and murmurs from the other bedroom ceased; Laurie's breathing continued evenly. Dan still lay wide awake.

He had never really noticed before how very dark everything could be. It was more than blackness; it seemed to fill space as water fills a pool. It seemed to fill the inside of his head.

He lay for some time with the darkness everywhere; then he got up very quietly. He put trousers and sweater on over his pyjamas, bunchily. Laurie's breathing never changed. He tiptoed out of the bedroom and downstairs. In the hall he put on his Wellington boots. He let himself out of the house and then through the front gate. There was no one about, no lights in the houses, except for a night light where a child slept. There was one lamp in the lane and that sent his shadow leaping horribly ahead of him. Then he turned a corner and the lamplight had gone. He was taking the short cut towards the river.

No moon tonight. No stars. Darkness . . .

He had been born here; he had always lived here; he knew these meadows as well as he knew himself;

but the darkness made him afraid. He could not see the familiar way ahead; he had to remember it. He felt his way. He scented it. He smelt the river before he came to it, and he felt the vegetation changing underfoot, growing ranker when he reached the bank.

He lowered himself into the water, from darkness into darkness. He began to feel along the roots of the bank for the up-ended brick. He found it quickly—he had not been far out in the point at which he had struck the bank.

His hand was on the brick, and he kept it there while he tried to see. In the darkness and through the darkness he tried to see what was going to happen—what he was going to make happen. What he was going to do.

Now that he was no longer moving, he could hear the sound of other movements in the darkness. He heard the water flowing. He heard a *drip* of water into water somewhere near him; a long pause; another *drip*. He heard a quick, quiet bird-call that was strange to him; certainly not an owl—he used to hear those as he lay snug in bed in his bedroom at home. And whatever sound he heard now, he heard beneath it the ceaseless watery whispering sound of the river, as if the river were alive and breathing in its sleep in the darkness, like Laurie left sleeping in the bedroom at home.

It was within his power to move the brick and take hold of the plastic carton and tip it right over. Fresh would fall into the water with a *plop* so tiny that he might never hear it above the flow of the river. In such darkness there would be no question of finding Fresh again, ever.

If he meant to do it, he could do it in three seconds. His hand was on the brick.

But did he mean to do it?

He tried to see what was in his mind, but his mind was like a deep pool of darkness. He didn't know what he really meant to do.

Suddenly he took his hand from the brick and stood erect. He put his booted foot on one of the lateral roots that extended behind the brick. He had to feel for it with his toe. Having found it, he pressed it slowly downwards; then quickly took his foot off again. He could feel the root, released from the pressure, following his foot upwards again in a little jerk.

That jerk of the root might have been enough to upset or at least tilt the carton. It might have been enough to tip Fresh out into the river.

On the other hand, of course, it might not have been enough.

Dan flung himself at the bank well to one side of the brick and clambered up and began a blundering run across the meadows. He did not slow up or go more carefully until he reached the lamplight of the lane and the possibility of someone's hearing his footsteps.

He let himself into the house and secured the door behind him. He left his boots in the hall and his clothes on the chair in the bedroom. He crept back into bed. Laurie was still breathing gently and regularly.

Dan slept late the next morning. He woke to bright sunshine flooding the room and Laurie banging on the bedrail: "Fresh! Fresh! Fresh!" he was chanting. Dan looked at him through eyes half-shut. He was trying to remember a dream he had had last night. It had been a dream of darkness—too dark to remember, or to want to remember. But when he went downstairs to breakfast and saw his boots in the hall with mud still drying on them, he knew that he had not dreamt last night.

Immediately after breakfast they went down to the river. Laurie was carrying his jam-jar.

They climbed down into the shallows as usual. Laurie made a little sound of dismay when he saw the brick: "It's lopsided—the current's moved it!"

Dan stood at a distance in the shallows while Laurie scrabbled the brick down into the water with a splash. There, behind it, was the white plastic carton, but at a considerable tilt, so that water flowed steadily from its lowest corner. "Oh, Fresh—Fresh!" Laurie implored, in a whisper. He was peering into the carton.

"Well?" said Dan, from his distance, not moving.

"Oh, no!" Laurie exclaimed, low but in dismay.

"Well?"

Laurie was poking with a finger at the bottom of the carton. Suddenly he laughed. "He's here after all! It's all right! It was just that burying trick of his! Fresh is here!"

Laurie was beaming.

Dan said, "I'm glad."

Laurie transferred Fresh from the carton to the jam-jar, together with some mud and stones and a suitable amount of river-water. Dan watched him.

Then they both set off across the meadows again,

Laurie holding the jam-jar carefully, as he would need to do—as he *would* do—during all the long journey to London. He was humming to himself. He stopped to say to Dan, "I say, I did thank you for Fresh, didn't I?"

"Don't thank me," said Dan.

Still Jim and Silent Jim

Old James Heslop came to live with his daughter-in-law when young Jim was still a baby. By then Mrs Heslop was a widow with four children—young Jim being the last. She was glad to take in old Jim to live with the family. It was true that he over-crowded an already crowded little house, and—since he could not get up and down stairs—he had to have the downstairs room which had the television set in it. On the other hand, he gave his daughter-in-law nearly all his Old Age Pension, as his share of the housekeeping expenses. Besides, Mrs Heslop, hard-worked and harassed and sharp-tongued even to her children, had a kind heart. "When you're old, you need a real home," she said. "This is Grandad's as long as he wants it."

Old Jim was less trouble than might have been supposed. Take the television set, for instance. He was not at all interested in watching television, but, as he was stone deaf, he did not mind the rest of the Heslop family having it on in his room. Indeed, as long as his chair was turned so that he need not look directly at the screen, he enjoyed it. "That makes a flickering on the walls, like firelight," he would remark. "And you don't always get the chance of an open fire to sit by these days."

Another convenience of old Jim's deafness was that he did not mind the noisiness of the three elder Heslop children; and of young Jim—who never said much anyway—he was very fond. It was a mutual affection. As soon as he could crawl, young Jim crawled round his grandfather's chair; and he first stood upright, rocking on unsteady legs, the better to listen to the deep, booming voice that was all the louder for old Jim's never hearing it himself. Young Jim listened before ever he could have understood what was being said; even later, he very rarely attempted a word in reply. In summer, old Jim's chair was put out into the front garden, and he sat in the sun, with his hands motionless on the rug over his knees, statue-like except for his jaw that moved when he spoke; and young Jim roamed about the flower-borders, listening but silent. That was how the pair got their nickname from the neighbours: Still Jim and Silent Jim.

Young Jim was so silent that the neighbours said privately that he must be simple-minded; but when he went to school he proved otherwise. He still spoke as little as possible, but he learnt as well as anyone.

Even before young Jim had learnt to read properly, he began bringing books home to show to his grandfather. The old man's eyesight was still good, and he read the text and looked at the pictures and told Silent Jim what he thought. Old Jim enjoyed books of history especially. He sighed and shook his head over them. "Ah! those days!" he said; and it cannot always have been very clear to young Jim whether those days had been his grandfather's, or days of long, long before his grandfather's birth. Old Jim pored over illustrations of the earliest motor-car and the penny-farthing bicycle, and before that the stage coach, and the pack-horse, and the Roman chariot—"Ah! those days—those days! And the men that lived then! Why, they were giants on the earth in those days!" The neighbours, overhearing the old man, would smile and tap their foreheads, for they were sure that if Silent Jim were not simple-minded, Still Jim had become so—at least, a little. The rest of the Heslop family did not believe it of their grandfather, but they paid no attention to him—that is, all except for young Jim: he listened closely, staring with eyes just the blue of his grandfather's but not yet faded with extreme age.

Old Jim had been over eighty when he moved into the Heslops' television room, so he must have been over ninety when young Jim was about ten. By then young Jim would occasionally—if necessary—start a conversation. One day he planted himself in front of his grandfather and said: "If you're over ninety, Grand-dad, you must be over sixty as well." He did not shout

—that would have been of no use; but he used an oddly still voice that seemed to creep into old Jim's ears in a way that no bawling could have done. Besides, he stood where the old man could watch his lips, and he shaped them very distinctly in speaking.

"Aye," said old Jim.

"Then you could belong to the Over Sixties' Club up the village," said young Jim, and cocked his head at him. Old Jim cocked his head back, and they stared at each other for a while.

"There's a boy at school," said young Jim, "his grand-dad goes. They play dominoes, they do, and whist. They have cups of tea, they do, and birthday parties. It's in the Church Hall."

"How'd I get there?" said old Jim.

"Oh!" said young Jim, and stared and pondered, and at last wandered away. This was before the time that the eldest Heslop girl took up with nice young Steve from the garage, who could hire a car very cheaply for his friends.

A day or two later young Jim came to his grand-father and said: "There's bath-chairs that belong to the Over Sixties' Club."

Old Jim nodded, as though to congratulate young Jim on a fine piece of investigation.

"They cost nothing," said young Jim.

Old Jim nodded, and stared at young Jim. This time young Jim nodded back.

No more was said on the subject, but the following Friday young Jim wheeled a bath-chair up to the Heslops' house and as near to the front doorstep as it could be got. Then he went in to fetch his grandfather.

Mrs Heslop came running, in agitation. "Whatever are you thinking of, Jim!" she cried. "You're never going to get your grandad into that chair—not with his heart—not with his joints—not at his age!"

"I'm going to the Over Sixties' Club," said old Jim. He threw aside his rug and, with a stick in one hand and the other hand on his grandson's shoulder, he struggled up out of his armchair.

When old Jim stood up, you saw that he was a tall old man—"six foot, even allowing for shrinkage," he always said; and then would add: "And my father was well over six foot, and my grandfather—that lies in the churchyard over in Little Barley—he was seven foot. You can see his tombstone there, like a giant's. Ah! those days!"

Now, seeing him determinedly on his feet, Mrs Heslop cried: "And look at yourself, Grandad! You're a big, heavy man, even if you are skin and bone! Young Jim can never push you all through the village to the Over Sixties' Club!"

"I can," said young Jim.

Old Jim reached the bath-chair and let himself down into it; young Jim lifted his legs in after him, and put the rug over them. Then they set off.

"Anyway, you're to be careful!" Mrs Heslop called after them. "You're to mind all that traffic on the London road!"

Great Barley, where the Heslops lived, was a busy, built-up village, with a main stream of traffic running through it on the way to London. "Not like the old days," said old Jim. "Great and Little Barley, they were both quiet then." Little Barley, being several miles away and quite off the main road, was still quiet. Hardly anyone went there.

Fortunately, to reach the Over Sixties' Club at the other end of Great Barley village, Silent Jim and Still Jim never had to cross the main road at all. They arrived safely.

The Chief Organiser welcomed them. She smiled in a kindly and congratulatory way at young Jim. "That must have been a long, hard push for a boy of your size. Now you must run off, and come back at five o'clock to take your grandfather home again. Children can't attend the Club."

Young Jim stared at the Chief Organiser, answered nothing and stood his ground. She said in a low voice to the other organisers, "I don't think he can understand." She turned to old Jim. "Your grandson..." she began.

Slowly he moved his hand up to cup it round his ear, and looked inquiring. "I'm deaf," he explained; "deaf as a post; deaf as a stone."

"Your grandson . . ." shouted the Chief Organiser.

Old Jim shook his head. "No, I shall never hear." He looked at her pleasantly. "But you mustn't think I'm unhappy. I'm very happy. If I have young Jim with me, I'm all right. Never you mind us."

The Chief Organiser gave up, and young Jim remained with his grandfather—the only child regularly to attend the Over Sixties' Club. He sat by old Jim, watching his play at dominoes, holding his saucer for him when he drank tea and picking the cake crumbs off his waistcoat. Young Jim himself drank tea and ate cake, but old Jim always paid for both of them, so that you could not say that the Club was cheated of anything. Moreover, young Jim kept the bath-chair (they always used the same one) in apple-pie order, brushing out the bottom, where old Jim put his feet, polishing the metalwork and oiling the little wheels in a vain attempt to get rid of their squeak. After a while, the Chief Organiser said the bath-chair might be kept in the Heslops' outhouse, which was done.

At about this time Maisie Heslop began her friendship with young Steve from the garage. He suggested that, one summer Sunday, he should take the family on a day's outing to the seaside; he would hire the car and drive.

All the Heslops went. Mrs Heslop sat at the front with Steve, and Maisie sat between them—she did not seem to mind being squeezed up a little. The other three children travelled at the back; and right across the back seat, underneath them all, travelled old Jim. It seemed hard on the old man—it was hard for them, too, because he was very bony—but he found it was the only way he could go in a car at all. "That's not a patch on a bath-chair", he whispered to young Jim; but what old Jim thought to be a whisper was something quite loud and clear. Everyone heard it; and Steve laughed, and Maisie went red with indignation.

Old Jim had to get into the car before the others, because he had great difficulty in bending his back and legs. First of all, he sat backwards on to the seat, and some of the Heslops went round to the other side and leaned into the car and pulled him, and the remainder of the Heslops stayed at his legs end and pushed him from there.

Old Jim puffed and groaned. "That's not worth it," he said. " 'Tisn't the way to travel—hemmed in—" (he knocked his head against the roof of the car) "—boxed down! That was different in the old days: carriages, and horses; room to move—fresh air! A bath-chair, now, that's a kind of carriage."

"You may like a bath-chair for some things," said Steve, "but it can't go as fast as a car."

"I've heard you say to young Jim that you wish sometimes he could push your bath-chair faster," said Mrs Heslop.

"You'll never go anywhere farther than your old Club, just in a bath-chair. In Steve's car we shall get to the seaside and back in a day," said Maisie.

Young Jim said nothing, because he never did; and the other two Heslop children were too busy pulling and pushing.

Old Jim said nothing, because he had heard nothing.

By now old Jim was completely in the back of the car; but cross-corneredly, with his right elbow against the window of the right-hand door, his left elbow against the back window and his toes turned up against the bottom of the left-hand door. He was in—just.

Having made sure that the door could be shut on him, the three younger Heslop children opened it again and climbed in on top of their grandfather. They sat where they could. Young Jim sat on old Jim's stomach, because someone had to sit there, and he was the lightest. Also he was his grandfather's favourite.

So they set off. When they reached the seaside, old Jim was pulled out of the car and put into a deck-chair. He was so breathless from the journey and so exhausted from getting in and out of the car that he dropped into sleep at once. He woke up for the picnic, and again to be put back into the car. When they got home and they were all thanking Steve and saying what a good driver he was and what a nice car and what a pleasant trip, old Jim said loudly: "Never again!"

"Grandad!" said Mrs Heslop reproachfully. "And after such a lovely day!"

"And Steve's having taken such trouble!" cried Maisie.

"Don't mind me," said Steve, for he really did not mind.

"They talk about modern improvements, I believe," said old Jim. "Some things are improvements; some aren't. Especially for people too old for them—or too big. I daresay I'm an old-fashioned size for travelling in a modern motor-car. What my grandfather would have done—he that was seven feet tall—broad too ..."

"It's not kind to Steve!" Maisie cried. "And I don't believe your old grandfather was seven feet high, so there!" And she burst into tears.

"What's she crying for?" asked old Jim. They all looked at young Jim to explain. He was silent, and Maisie went on crying.

"What did she say?" asked old Jim. "Nobody tells me anything nowadays; for some reason nobody speaks to me—except young Jim. Come on, Jim, you tell me what she said."

Young Jim looked uncertain, but he said: "She says it's not kind to Steve." Old Jim looked dumbfounded. "And she says she doesn't believe your grandfather was seven feet high, so there."

Old Jim put his head back, closing his eyes, as though he were too tired to speak. At last he said: "So that's what's behind it. They've never believed me. Everything's modern nowadays, and everybody's young and small; and they all believe that's the right thing, and the only thing, and that it was never any different. They don't believe in those old days."

"O Grandad!" said Maisie, and began crying in a different way. "I didn't mean that. Young Jim, tell him I didn't really mean that."

"Grandad!" said young Jim, and took the old man's hand and shook it gently until he opened his eyes. "Grandad, she says she didn't mean it."

"They don't mean me to know what they think," said old Jim; "but they think it all the same."

There was nothing more to be said. Maisie went on crying for some time; but, on her mother's advice, she did not speak of the subject again.

The next time that Steve brought the car round to take the Heslops on a jaunt—to Whipsnade Zoo this time, to see the animals—old Mr Heslop said he would stay at home. Maisie made him egg sandwiches for his tea, and kissed him goodbye remorsefully. Silent Jim stayed with him, although he, too, loved to see strange animals.

The summer advanced. Every Friday young Jim pushed his grandfather's bath-chair through the village to the Over Sixties' Club. Then the organisers decided to close the Club for the month of August, because most people went on their holidays then. The Heslops could not really afford a holiday; but Steve from the garage took Maisie and the two middle children off to a seaside camp for a fortnight. Mrs Heslop did not go: she said it would be holiday enough to be left in the house with three less children than usual. Old Jim did not go, because he said he didn't want to; and young Jim would not go, even at his mother's urging. He would not say why, but his grandfather looked at him sadly: "You'd have enjoyed the sea." Young Jim neither assented nor contradicted. "You shouldn't have stayed for me," said old Jim.

Young Jim thought that old Jim might be lonely; and old Jim worried that young Jim might be dull. Every day of that hot season the neighbours saw them out in the front garden of the Heslops' house, in what shade there was: Silent Jim busy with some job of his own making, and Still Jim talking to him. Since the time of his unhappy return from the day by the sea, the old man had not referred again to "those days". Now, however, alone with young Jim, he felt free to go back into his memory for stories to interest and amaze. He would always end by saying: "And that was true, for all there's nothing left to prove it, and people disbelieve."

One late afternoon he had been talking in this strain for some time. They had finished their tea; and young Jim had got the bath-chair out and was cleaning the wickerwork with an old toothbrush. Mrs Heslop came out to fetch their tea-things, and said: "It's a pity there's nowhere to take your grandad in the bath-chair, till the Club opens again next month." She went in again to do the bit of washing-up.

Old Jim had stopped talking, and he did not start again now. Young Jim looked up at him in surprise.

His grandfather beckoned to him to come close. "If I speak like this," he said, "can anyone hear but you?"

Young Jim looked round carefully. There were no neighbours in the gardens, and his mother was in the kitchen with the taps running. He shook his head.

His grandfather put his hand up and pulled young Jim's head into such a position that the boy's ear was only a few inches away from his mouth when he spoke. "What would you say to a jaunt—a real pleasure-jaunt?"

Silent Jim turned his face so that his grandfather could see his eyebrows going up.

Old Jim nodded. "Mind you, it's a long push with the bath-chair."

Silent Jim simply left his eyebrows up.

"It came to me just now, in a flash," said old Jim. "The whole plan. We'll go over to Little Barley, where I was born, where I was christened at the font in the church there, with my father and grandfather standing by—my grandfather that's buried in the same church-yard—he that was seven foot tall. I'll show it to you—all of it."

Young Jim said: "When?"

"The sooner the safer, before the weather thinks to break. Tomorrow; and very early in the morning, before the traffic's on the main road, at least for our first crossing of it; and before others are about. Before your mother wakes."

Silent Jim nodded emphatically.

"Sunrise is before five now," said old Jim. "I've often seen it, for at my age I sleep lightly, and never late."

It was easy for old Jim to wake early, but a different matter for young Jim; and it would be impossible for his grandfather to call to him without waking Mrs Heslop too, or to get upstairs in order to wake him quietly.

Young Jim's bedroom upstairs, like old Jim's room on the ground floor, was at the front of the house. This gave young Jim his idea. That evening he made a very long length of string out of several shorter pieces knotted together. The string stretched from his bedroom, out through the window, down and in again at the window of his grandfather's room. The lower end was left within easy reach of old Jim's hand; the upper end was tied round young Jim's big toe. The device was put into working position after Mrs Heslop had gone to bed; and the next morning—before morning seemed even to have come—it worked perfectly.

That summer dawn surprised young Jim by its stillness and greyness: he had expected at least reds and yellows in the sky, like a festival. He was surprised, too, at the chill in the air, even indoors, at this time of heat-wave. He dressed his grandfather in his warmest clothes, and gave him an extra rug for the bath-chair. They had not planned to have any breakfast at all, but now young Jim—who was a sensible boy—saw they would need something later to warm them. The most that he dared do was to boil a kettle and make a thermos flask of tea. He also put a handful of digestive biscuits into a paper bag. "And," said old Jim, in his lowest voice, "we'll take your mother's tape-measure." He would not say why.

With old Jim in the bath-chair, and the flask and biscuits and the tape-measure on his knees, they left the house. In all the houses they passed the curtains were still drawn; none of the neighbours was up. Young Jim pushed the bath-chair along with his heart in his mouth, for the squeak of the wheels sounded very loud in the morning silence. Perhaps, if anyone heard at all, the hearer thought it was only the early, monotonous call of some strange bird.

They left the housing-estate and came out on to the main road. There was no traffic at all to be seen, until an all-night lorry rumbled by. Then nothing again.

They crossed the main road unhurriedly and without the slightest danger, and struck off down the road to Little Barley. Now that they were leaving the houses of Great Barley behind them, old Jim dared talk aloud; and young Jim, feeling that they were really on their way, relaxed his pace and looked around him as he went.

This was a country road, going always deeper into the country. There were wide verges where the grasses grew tall, yellowing and drying with the heats of August. There were few flowers left in bloom; but the plants in the ditches were fresh and green where they could still suck up refreshment and life from ditch-water or ditch-mud.

Dew lay on grasses and plants and hedges—a short-lived coolness before the sun should come again in its full strength. Already young Jim began to feel its warmth on his back; and bath-chair and bath-chair-pusher together began to make a strange long shadow on the road ahead.

They came to a bridge over a river and crossed it; they skirted a high wall—old Jim made young Jim stop to look at a fading black mark on it. When he was a young man, old Jim said, that mark had been repainted yearly: it was the boundary-sign between the parishes of Great and Little Barley. When he was a boy, the champion fighter of the two villages stood with a foot on either side of the mark and shouted:

> Barley Little and Barley Great,
> Here I stand and won't be beat.

They went on, and crossed a railway line, where you opened the gate for yourself and had to look both ways for safety.

They reached the outskirts of Little Barley village— a cluster of cottages and a farmhouse, and the church beyond. They still saw no sign of anyone astir and heard no sound of life, except a clank of metal from a farm-building—perhaps a bucket in a cowshed where the early milking was starting.

They came to the little grey church. Young Jim pushed the bath-chair up the path between the tombstones, to the church door. The door might so easily have been locked, but it was not. Young Jim could have wheeled the bath-chair right inside, but old Jim thought that it might not be respectful. He got out of the chair instead, and, leaning on young Jim's shoulder, he hobbled inside.

Little Barley was such a small village that no rector or vicar lived in it, and services were held in the church only occasionally. You could feel that on entering. There was a silence that was surprised to be disturbed. Church spiders had spun threads across and across the aisles, from pew-head to pew-head. Young Jim felt them breaking across his body as he and his grandfather paced along.

Now they were facing the east end of the church and the altar. Behind and above it was a great window of pale greenish glass, through which streamed the light of the risen sun.

Old Jim blinked into the light, and his eyes filled with tears, and he sat down rather suddenly in the pew beside him, and prayed.

When he had finished, he said to young Jim: "I was married to your grandmother at that altar. She died long before you were born." Then he took young Jim to the west end of the church, to the grey stone font. "I was christened here; my mother and father stood here for my christening. They're dead and gone too."

"And your grandfather stood with them," said young Jim. "He that was seven foot high."

"Aye, and he's gone, too." But this reminded old Jim of something. "I'll show you, outside," he said, "towards the east end of the church, it would be—his grave."

They went outside again, and, as old Jim was tired, he got back into the bath-chair and young Jim wheeled him along the narrow path that went round the outside of the church. Towards the east end of the churchyard, old Jim said, "Stop!" He looked round him. "You'll find it about here. James Heslop, his name was—like my name—like yours."

Young Jim began to look. The graves in this part of the churchyard were very old, overgrown and weather-worn. The inscriptions were hard to read.

Old Jim saw his grandson's difficulty. "Look for a big tombstone—the biggest. Seven foot tall he was, and his tombstone was to match."

"This is the longest tombstone," said young Jim at

last. He scraped away the ivy tendrils from the head of it. "There's an O here—no, it's a cherub's face. But there's writing below. I can't read the first letters, but here's an S, and an L, and this really is an O . . ."

"'Tis Heslop," said old Jim. "It's his. Wheel me close, boy."

Young Jim brought the bath-chair alongside the tombstone. Old Jim leant forward with the tape-measure he had brought. He placed one end at the head of the tombstone and, with difficulty, stretched the length of it out. It was only a five-foot tape-measure, and it did not reach. Young Jim had to measure the remainder separately.

"Five feet," he said, "and another two feet nine inches."

"Nearly eight foot," said old Jim, and lay back in his chair and closed his eyes. "You must tell your sister that; you must tell them all that. Nearly eight feet his tombstone had to be, because in his life he was seven foot tall. There's his tombstone to prove it. Seven foot tall—they were giants in those days."

Then he opened his eyes again and said briskly: "What about the tea?"

Young Jim set the thermos flask and the biscuits out on the tombstone, as his grandfather told him. "He would never have minded," said old Jim, "any more than I should mind if you did it to me, when I'm gone. No, I should take it kindly."

They took turns at drinking out of the cup-top of the thermos flask, and ate digestive biscuits. The time was still not yet half-past six, but there was no doubt that the day was going to be another scorcher. The sun warmed them as they breakfasted, and old Jim spread his handkerchief over the top of his head for protection. Bees came out and began work among the tall weeds of the churchyard. A robin suddenly appeared at the far end of the tombstone, and young Jim threw him some biscuit crumbs.

Unexpectedly, a car passed: they just saw its roof over the top of the churchyard wall, and then—for a second—the whole of it as it passed the gap that was the churchyard gate. Then they heard brakes go on; the car seemed to stop abruptly, and then it backed until it was by the gate again, and then it stopped again. After a moment two policemen got out, and stared at them.

"Who's got a better right than we have?" said old Jim indignantly. "It's my grandfather's tombstone."

The policemen opened the churchyard gate and began walking up the path.

Old Jim and young Jim watched them.

The policemen left the main path and, in single file, came along the narrow path by the church, directly towards the Heslops.

When he was still some way away, the policeman in front called out, in an arresting voice: "James Heslop!" That he knew their name seemed ominous.

He did not go on at once—it was as if words failed him; but the second policeman burst out: "Whatever are you doing here, James Heslop, with your daughter-in-law and your mother off her head looking for you?"

The policemen now began to talk both at once.

"Running round the village looking for you," said the first policeman.

"In her dressing-gown," said the second policeman.

"Came to us in despair," said the first policeman.

"In her bedroom slippers," said the second policeman.

"And here we've been looking for you ever since," said the first policeman. "Now, what were you two up to?"

Both policemen waited for an answer to this. Neither old Jim nor young Jim said anything, so the second policeman said, "Eh?"

Old Jim smiled and shook his head, and young Jim cast his eyes down, putting himself out of the conversation altogether.

The second policeman said suddenly: "The old 'un's deaf—you remember she said so; and she said the child couldn't be got to talk much."

"Deaf?" said the first policeman. He drew a deep breath into his great chest, so that the blue bulk of it advanced until the silver buttons, moving from sunlight to sunlight, twinkled. With his breath very slowly going out, in a voice that might have wakened seven-foot James Heslop under his tombstone, the policeman shouted: "We've come to take you home in the car, Mr Heslop." He added, with less voice—because he had less voice left: "The child can push the bath-chair back, empty." The policeman, when he had finished, looked tired and hollow-chested; old Jim smiled and shook his head.

"Deaf," said the second policeman.

Then the two policemen began to explain to old Jim, by gestures, what they intended. In dumb show they explained to him how they would help him into their car, and how comfortable he would be; they acted to him how swiftly and smoothly they would drive off—how soon they would get him safely home. Then they stopped to make sure he had understood. Old Jim clapped his hands and smiled; but he also shook his head.

The policemen started all over again, but, in the middle of their performance, one of them—perhaps losing patience—set his hands on the bath-chair as if to push it towards the car, with or without old Jim's permission. Then old Jim spoke, languidly—almost feebly: "I never like to be awkward, but I wouldn't like you to take on the responsibility of trying to get me into a car at my age. My joints are stiff, you know. And then there's my heart."

The policemen looked at old Jim carefully. He certainly appeared very frail, and he sounded very frail indeed. Yet they had promised Mrs Heslop not only to find her father-in-law and her son, but to bring the old man home at once.

"Yet I'd like to be home too," said old Jim. "It's been a strain—at my age—so early in the morning—so far . . ." He let his voice die away, and closed his eyes.

"We should get him home somehow, quickly," said the first policeman, and the second nodded; they both looked anxious.

In the anxious silence, old Jim suddenly said, "Ah!" so that both policemen jumped. He had opened his eyes, and now he said: "You could tow me home."

"Tow you home?" repeated the policemen.

"Fasten my bath-chair to the back of your car with

a tow-rope," said old Jim. "Pull me home on a tow-rope."

The policemen looked at each other, neither ever having been asked to tow anyone in a bath-chair before or heard of such a thing being done.

"It'd be a question for the Traffic Department, probably," said the first policeman.

"There'd be rules and regulations about it," said the second.

"For instance, he'd have to have his own number plate," said the first.

"Aye, he'd have been turned into a trailer."

Old Jim, not being able to follow the policemen's conversation, but seeing their hesitation, became impatient. "If you haven't a tow-rope, handcuffs would do. You could handcuff the bath-chair to the back of the car. Surely you have handcuffs in a police car."

"But you'd be a trailer!" shouted the first policeman.

"I'd be *what*?" asked old Jim—it was not clear whether he had not heard, or could not believe what he had heard.

The first policeman shook his head despairingly. "And it wouldn't be safe, anyway," he said.

"Unless, of course," said the second policeman, "we drove very slowly and carefully." He seemed to see possibilities in the idea after all.

"There is that," the first policeman agreed. "But, however you look at it, he'd be a trailer: I doubt it wouldn't be legal."

At this point, young Jim surprised them by speaking. "But nobody'd see."

It was quite true: the hour was still so early that there

was small danger of anybody's being on the roads between Little and Great Barley. On the other hand, the
likelihood of such an encounter increased with every
minute that the day advanced. If they were to act at all,
they must act quickly.

The second policeman persuaded the first. It turned
out, anyway, that they always carried a good rope in the
boot. With this they fastened the front of the bath-chair
—with old Jim still in it—to the back of the police car.
Young Jim tucked his grandfather well into the chair,
and then got into the back of the car. One policeman
sat with him, and the other drove.

They went very slowly—that is, for a car, but much
more quickly than a bath-chair could ever have been
pushed. From the beginning to the end of the journey
young Jim and the policeman with him kept watch
through the rear window. Young Jim pressed his nose
against the glass until it went white like a piece of
pastry, and his eyes were very anxious.

At first old Jim looked anxious too; but the faster he
went the more confident he seemed to become. His
white hair streamed in the wind, and he began to signal
to the two at the back for the car to go faster still. They
did not pass his message on to the driver. Already the
bath-chair was travelling at a speed it had never dreamt
of before: its whizzing wheels gave out an unbroken,
high-pitched squeak. "There'll be an accident!" the
wheels screamed. "An accident!"

There was no accident; nor were they observed by
anyone—unless you counted a horse looking over a
gate beyond Little Barley. He watched their coming,
but, when they were almost level with him, his nerve

seemed to break, for he galloped off, with his back hooves wildly in the air. Old Jim waved to him with one hand, clinging to the side of the bath-chair with the other.

Not even in Great Barley were there people about, or traffic.

They turned into the housing-estate, and the only sign of life was a figure drooping over one of the front gates: Mrs Heslop, waiting. The police car drew up beside her, and she looked at it, and at young Jim's face at the window, and at old Jim in the bath-chair behind. He was waving to her; and, now that the car engine was turned off, they could hear that he was singing—had probably been singing all the way. "Hearts of Oak" it must have been, because he now broke off at "Steady, boys, steady!"

Young Jim got out of the car quickly, and said: "Mum, I've come all the way from Little Barley in a police car!"

Mrs Heslop shot out an arm—perhaps to catch him to her, perhaps to slap him; but instead of doing either she suddenly put both hands up to her face and burst into tears.

Poor Mrs Heslop! Already it had been a long and very trying morning for her. She had not been woken at dawn by the gentle sounds of their setting forth; but a little later, waking of her own accord, she had listened to the silence of the house, and it had suddenly seemed to her unnatural in a way that it had never seemed before. She told herself that she was being foolish, and she tried to sleep again; but, in the end, she had got up and looked into young Jim's bedroom, and found him gone. Then she had found old Jim gone, and the bath-chair too. Then she had started out wildly to look for them, and had only been sent home by the comforting promises of the police. Since then she had waited at the gate.

One policeman unhitched old Jim's bath-chair, while the other put his arm round Mrs Heslop's shoulder and told her there was no need to cry now: everyone was safe and sound.

They all went indoors, and Mrs Heslop recovered sufficiently to boil a kettle and make a pot of tea. The policemen stayed to drink a cup, and then went off; and then Mrs Heslop settled down to cooking a proper, hot breakfast for old Jim and young Jim. "*Digestive biscuits!*" she snorted; and she served them with porridge and fried eggs and bacon and hot toast and marmalade, and more tea.

After breakfast, old Jim said that he was not really tired after all, and that he would like to sit out in the shade, in his usual chair, at the front of the house; and young Jim made him comfortable there. Young Jim wanted to stay with him, but Mrs Heslop put her foot down and made him go upstairs to bed, where—sure enough—he was soon falling asleep.

Mrs Heslop saw him into bed and drew his curtains against the bright sunlight, and left him: it was never much use, she knew, to question young Jim. She went downstairs and into the front garden. She planted herself in front of her father-in-law, so that he could not but pay some attention to her.

"Grandad!" she shouted. "Why did you *do* it?"

Old Jim nodded at her, and said: "And I hope they're

having as good weather by the seaside. I've something
to tell young Maisie, too, when she comes back. That
reminds me . . ." He reached into his pocket and
brought out the tape-measure. "Here's your tape-
measure that we borrowed, my dear."

He held it out to Mrs Heslop, and she took it, but as
in a dream of amazement, and carelessly. She only held
it by one end, so that the rest of the tape fell and rolled
round her feet, encircling them.

Mrs Heslop stared at the tape-measure and then at
old Jim. "But why, Grandad—why—why . . .?"

"Aye," said the old man, "those days..." He laughed
to himself. "But what my grandfather would have said
to see me bowling along this morning! The best of
both worlds—that's what I've had."

"You and young Jim . . ." said Mrs Heslop wonder-
ingly, still standing within her magic circle of tape,
staring at him. No longer was she expecting or hoping
to be heard; but, oddly, this time old Jim must partly
have heard her.

"Aye, he's a good boy." He blinked sleepily into the
sunlight. "And, you know, although he's not big for his
age, maybe he has the makings of a big man in him."
His eyelids drooped, then rose again. "Maybe he'll grow
to be six foot, after all, like his grandfather." Old Jim
settled himself into his chair: he was going to sleep, and
he knew it. "Or even seven foot, maybe, like his great-
great-grandfather." His eyelids fell again. He slept.

Upstairs in his bedroom, listening in his half-sleep
to the booming voice from outside, young Jim had
begun dreaming of giants and police cars.

The Great Blackberry-Pick

Dad was against waste—waste of almost anything: electricity, time, crusts of bread. Wasted food was his special dread. Just after the summer holidays, nearing the second or third Saturday of term: "Sun now," he would say, "frost later; and pounds and pounds and pounds and pounds of blackberries out in the hedges going to waste. Good food wasted: bramble jelly"— their mother flinched, perhaps remembering stained bags hanging from hooks in the kitchen—"jelly, and jam, and blackberry-and-apple pies . . ." He smacked his lips. Dad seemed to think he must mime enjoyment to make them understand.

Val said eagerly, "I love blackberries."

Her father beamed on her.

Chris said, "I don't. I don't like the pips between my teeth."

"Worse under your plate," their mother murmured.

Like their mother, Dad had false teeth, but he did not acknowledge them. He said scornfully, "In *bought* jam the pips are artificial. Tiny chips of wood. Put in afterwards."

"Nice job, carving 'em to shape," said Chris.

Peter was not old enough to think that funny, and Val decided not to laugh; so nobody did.

Peter said, "Do we have to go?"

"Bicycles," said Dad. "Everyone on bicycles and off into the country, blackberry-picking. Five of us should gather a good harvest."

"I'll make the picnic," Val said. She liked that kind of thing. She looked anxiously round her family. Their mother had turned her face away from them to gaze out of the window. Peter and Chris had fixed their eyes upon Dad: Peter would have to go, although much bicycling made his legs ache; but Chris, the eldest of them, as good as grown up—Chris said: "I'm not coming."

"Oh, Chris!" Val cried.

Dad said: "Not coming?"

"No."

"And why not?"

"I've been asked to go somewhere else on Saturday. I'm doing something else. I'm not coming."

No one had ever said that to Dad before. What would happen? Dad began to growl in his throat like a dog preparing to attack. Then the rumble died away. Dad said: "Oh, have it your own way then."

So that was one who wouldn't go blackberrying this year.

Nor did their mother go. When Saturday came, she didn't feel well, she said. She'd stay at home and have their tea ready for them.

Two fewer didn't matter, because Dad begged the two Turner children from next door. Mrs Turner was glad to be rid of them for the day, and they had bicycles.

"Bicycles," said Dad, "checked in good order, tyres pumped, brakes working, and so on. Then, the picnic." Val smiled and nodded. "Something to gather the blackberries in," went on Dad. "Not paper bags or rubbishy receptacles of that sort. Baskets, plastic carrier bags, anything like that. Something that will go into a bicycle basket, or can be tied on somewhere. Something that will bear a weight of blackberries. Right?"

Val said, "Yes," so that Dad could go on: "All assemble in the road at nine thirty. I'll have the map."

There they were on this fine Saturday morning in September at half past nine: Val and Peter and their dad and the two Turner children from next door, all on bicycles.

They had about four miles on the main road, riding very carefully, two by two or sometimes in single file, with Dad in the rear shouting to them. Then Dad directed them to turn off the main road into a side road, and after that it was quiet country roads all the way. As Chris had once said, you had to hand it to Dad: Dad was good with a map; he knew where he was going.

Country roads; and then lanes that grew doubtful of

themselves and became mere grassy tracks. These were the tracks that, in the old days, people had made on foot or on horseback, going from one village to the next. Nowadays almost no one used them.

They were pushing their bikes now, or riding them with their teeth banging in their gums. The Turner children each fell off once, and one cried.

"Quiet now!" Dad said severely, as though the blackberries were shy wild creatures to be taken by surprise.

They left their bicycles stacked against each other and followed Dad on foot, walking steeply through an afforestation of pines, and then out into a large clearing, on a hillside, south-facing, and overgrown with brambles.

You had to hand it to Dad, it was a marvellous place.

The bushes were often more than a man's height and densely growing, but with irregular passages between them. The pickers could edge through narrow gaps or stoop under stems arched to claw and clutch. For most of the time they wore their anoraks with the hoods up.

The blackberries grew thickly. They were very big and ripe—many already over-ripe, with huge bluebottles squatting on them.

"Eat what you want, to begin with," said Dad. "Soon enough you won't want to eat any more. Then just pick and go on picking." He smiled. He was good-tempered. Everything was going well.

They separated at once, to pick. They went burrowing about among the bushes, meeting each other, exclaiming, drawn to each other's blackberry clumps, because always someone else's blackberries seemed bigger, riper.

They picked and picked and picked and picked. Their teeth and tongues and lips were stained, but their fingers were stained the most deeply, because they went on picking—on and on and on—after they had stopped eating. Dad had been right about that, too. But himself, he never ate any blackberries at all; just picked.

The brambles scratched them. Val had a scratch on her forehead that brought bright blood oozing down into her eyebrow. "Nothing!" said Dad. He tied her head with a handkerchief to stop the bleeding. The handkerchief had been a present to him; it was red with white spots. When he had tied it round Val's head, he called her his pirate-girl.

Then he looked into her plastic carrier bag. "Why, pirate-girl, you've picked more blackberries than anyone else!"

When Dad had gone off again, Peter began to dance round Val: "Pirate-girl! Pirate-girl!" Val didn't mind; no, she really enjoyed it. She felt happy to have picked more blackberries than anyone else, and for Dad to have said so, and to be wearing Dad's handkerchief and to be teased for what he had called her. The Turner children appeared round a bramble corner, and she was glad of the audience. Peter was good-humoured, too. His legs had stopped aching, and he had forgotten that they would ache again. The children were in early afternoon sunshine and blackberry-scented air; they had picked enough blackberries to be proud of; the picnic would be any time now; and Dad was in a good temper.

"Pirate-girl!" Peter teased. He set down his basket of blackberries to pick a solitary stem of hogweed, dry and straight and stiff. With this he made cutlass-slashes at Val.

There was no weapon to hand for Val, so she used her carrier-bag to parry him. She swung the bag to and fro, trying to bang his stem and break it. The weight in the carrier made it swing slowly, heavily, like a pendulum. Val was getting nowhere in the fight, but she was enjoying it. She hissed fiercely between her teeth. Peter dodged. The bag swung.

Dad came back round the bushes and saw them. Val couldn't stop the swinging at once; and at once an awful thing began to happen. The swinging was too much for the weight of the blackberries in the bag. The bottom did not fall out—after all, the bag was plastic; but the plastic where she gripped it began to stretch. The handle-holes elongated swiftly and smoothly. Swiftly and smoothly the plastic round them thinned, thinned out into nothingness. No ripping, no violent severance; but the bag gave way.

The blackberries shot out at Dad's feet. They pattered impudently over his Wellington boots; nestled there in a squashy heap. Val, looking down at them, knew they were wasted. She had gathered them, and she had literally thrown them away. She lifted her eyes to Dad's face: his brows were heavy, his lips open and drawn back, his teeth showed, ground together.

Then he growled, in his way.

She turned and ran. She ran and ran, as fast as she could, to get away. Fast and far she ran: now, as she ran, there were pine-trees on either side of her, an audience that watched her. Then she tripped and fell painfully over metal, and realised that she had reached the bicycles. She pulled her own bicycle from the heap and got on it and rode. The way was downhill and rough, and she was riding too fast for carefulness. She was shaken violently as though someone were shaking a wicked child.

She followed the track by which they had come; then diverged into another. The way grew smoother; she passed a farm-house; the surface under her wheels was made up now. She took another turn and another, and was in a narrow road between high hedges. She cycled on and came to a cross-roads: two quiet country roads quietly meeting and crossing, with no signpost saying anything. Without consideration she took the turn towards the downward sloping of the sun, and cycled on more slowly. She knew that she was lost, and she was glad of it.

She found that she had a headache. She was surprised at the headache, and wondered if the tight-tied handkerchief had caused it. Then she connected the feeling in her head with a feeling in her stomach: she was hungry. They had all been hungry for the picnic even before the pirate-fight, and she had ridden away without eating.

She was so tired and hungry that she cried a little as she pedalled along. She knew she had nearly twenty pence in the pocket of her anorak. She could buy herself some food.

But these were not roads with shops on them. Another farm; a derelict cottage; and suddenly a bungalow with a notice at the gate: "Fruit. Veg."

She leant her bicycle against the hedge and went up the path towards the front-door. But the front-door had a neglected look, and a motor-mower was parked right against it, under the shelter of the porch. She turned and went round the side of the bungalow, following a path but also a faint, enticing smell. The smell grew stronger, more exciting. The side-door she came to was also a kitchen-door, and it stood ajar. From inside came a smell of roast meat and of delicious baking.

Val went right up to the door and peered in. The kitchen was empty of people. A meal had just been finished. A baby's high chair stood near the table, its tray spattered with mashed potato and gravy. There was no food left on the table except more mashed potato and the remains of a treacle-tart in a baking tin.

And there was the smell, overwhelming now.

Val inhaled and looked.

A door opened and a young woman came into the kitchen. She picked up the tin with the treacle-tart in it, evidently to put it away somewhere. Then she saw Val's face at the crack of the door. She gave a gasp.

Val pushed the door wide open to show how harmless she was, and with the same intention said, "I saw the notice at the gate."

"Oh," said the woman, recovering, "that shouldn't be there still. Should have come down last week. We've not much stuff left, you see. What did you want? Vegetable marrow?"

"Something to eat now," said Val. The woman had put the treacle-tart down on the table again.

"Blackberries?" the woman suggested.

"No," said Val. "Not blackberries. Thank you."

The woman had been staring at her. "Why's your head tied up? Have you had an accident? You're very pale."

"No," said Val. "I'm all right really." The woman's hand was still on the treacle-tart tin; she remained staring.

"You have had an accident."

"Not really." Val didn't want to think of what had happened among the brambles. "I fell off my bike."

The woman left the treacle-tart and came across to Val. She slipped the handkerchief from her head and laid it aside. She examined Val's brow. "It's really only a scratch, but it's bled a lot. You sit down." She cleaned the wound and then dressed it with a plaster. Then, "You'd better have some tea. I was going to make a pot while the baby slept." She boiled the kettle and made the tea. She also cleared the kitchen table, taking the treacle-tart away and shutting it into a larder. Val watched it go, over the cup of tea the woman poured for her.

Next the woman opened the oven-door just a crack. A smell of baking, hot, dry, delicious, came out and made straight for Val. The woman was peering into the oven: "Ah," she said. "Yes." She opened the oven-door wide and took out two tin trays of scones, done to a turn. She got out a wire rack and began to transfer the scones one by one from the trays to the rack. They were so hot that she picked each one up by the tips of her fingers and very quickly.

"Have another cup," she said hospitably to Val.

"I won't have any more to drink, thank you," Val said. The scones sat on their wire rack, radiating heat and smell. The woman finished with the trays and began washing up.

There were footsteps outside and a young man appeared, carrying a pig-bucket. He left it just outside and came in. "Hello!" he said to Val. "Where've you sprung from?"

"She fell off her bike. I've given her a cup of tea." The woman dried her hands. "You might like a scone, too?"

Val nodded. She couldn't say anything.

The woman slit a scone, buttered it and handed it to her.

"What about me?" asked the man.

"You!" said the woman. From the rack she chose a scone misshapen but huge, made from the last bits of dough clapped together. She slit it, pushed a hunk of butter inside and gave it to him.

"Would you like another?" she asked Val.

Val said she would. The woman watched her eating the second scone. "Haven't you had much dinner?"

Val didn't decide what she was going to say. It came at once: 'The others all rode away from me when I fell off my bike. Rode off with the picnic."

The woman was indignant. "But didn't you try to catch up with them again?"

"I got lost."

The woman gave Val a third scone and her husband a second. She went to the larder and came back with the treacle-tart, which she set before Val. "There's a nice surprise for you," she said.

They asked where Val lived, and when she told them, the man said, "Quite a way on a bike."

Val said, "If you could tell me how to get to the main

road from here. All these lanes, and not many sign-posts . . ."

"Tricky," said the man.

Then the woman said, "Weren't you taking the van to the garage some time to get that part?"

"Ah," said the man. "Yes. I could set her on her way. Room for the bike in the back."

"No hurry," the woman said to Val. "You sit there."

Away somewhere a baby began to cry and the woman went to fetch it. While she was out of the kitchen, the man helped himself to another scone and butter, winking at Val. The woman came back with the baby in her arms. "You!" she said to the man. He kissed her with his mouth full of scone, and kissed the baby.

The woman said to Val: "You hold her while I finish the washing-up." So Val held the baby, smelling of cream cheese and warm woollies and talcum powder. The baby seemed to like her.

"Well," the man said to Val, "I'll be back for you later."

His wife gave him the old mashed potato and other remains for the pig-bucket. "It wasn't worth your coming for it specially," she said.

"No," he said. "But I remembered about the scones."

"You!" she said.

He laughed and went off with his pig-bucket again.

Val nursed the baby, and gave it a rusk, and helped to change its nappies, and played with it. The mother cleared and cleaned the kitchen and washed out the nappies.

It all took some time. Then the man came again.

"Ready?" he said to Val. Val took her anorak, that the

baby had been sucking, and went with him. He had already hoisted the bicycle into the back of the van. The woman came to the gate with the baby in her arms. The baby slapped at the notice saying: "Fruit. Veg." "You never get round to taking that notice down," the woman said to her husband. He grunted, busy with the van. Val kissed goodbye to the baby, who took a piece of her cheek and twisted it.

Then Val got into the van and they drove off. Val was not noticing the way they took; she was thinking of the warm, sweet-smelling kitchen they had left. As they drove along, she half-thought they passed one of the two farm-houses she had noticed earlier when she was cycling; but that was all.

She began to think of what it would be like when she got home.

They reached the main road at last and drove along it a short way to the garage. Here the man lifted Val's bicycle out of the van, and she mounted it. He gave her clear directions to set her on her way, ending with, "You should be home well before dusk."

So she was; and they were all waiting for her. Even Chris was there. The Turner children had wanted to stay, too, but Dad had packed them off home.

There was a great explosion from Dad about what had happened at the blackberry-pick and after. Val was given some tea, but the row from Dad went on during it and after it. Their mother started her ironing; Chris settled down to TV; Peter played a quiet but violent game with soldiers and tanks behind the couch. Dad went on and on.

"And what about that sticking-plaster?" he shouted

suddenly. Their mother knocked the iron against the ironing-board, almost toppling it. "Where's my red handkerchief that I lent you?"

In a flash of memory Val saw the red handkerchief laid aside on the dresser in that scone-smelling, baby-smelling kitchen. "A woman gave me a cup of tea," she said. "She took the handkerchief off and put the plaster on instead. I must have left the handkerchief there."

"My red handkerchief!" Dad shouted.

"Oh," muttered Chris, without taking his eyes off TV, "a red cotton handkerchief!"

"I'm sorry," Val said to Dad.

"Sorry!"

Then Dad cross-questioned her: who was this woman, and where did she live? All Val could say was that she lived quite a way from the bramble-patch and from the main road, in a bungalow with a notice at the gate saying: "Fruit. Veg."

"Right," said Dad. "You'll come with me tomorrow. You'll cycle back the way you came. You'll help me search until we find that bungalow and the woman and my red handkerchief."

So the next day—Sunday—Val cycled with her father alone into the country. Just the two of them: once she would have loved that.

He led them systematically to and fro among the country lanes. ("Do you recognise this road? Could that be the bungalow? Look, girl, *look*!") Dad knew his map and he was thorough in his criss-crossing of the countryside; but they saw few bungalows, and none with a notice at the gate saying: "Fruit. Veg."

As they passed one bungalow, Val looked up the

path to the front-door. Against it, under the shelter of the porch, was parked a motor-mower. Also a pole with a board at the top; the inscription on the board faced the front-door. And behind the glass of a window Val thought she saw movement—the odd, top-heavy shape of someone carrying a child. But they were cycling past too quickly for her to be sure.

When they got home at last, Dad was too tired to go on with the row. He just said: "A day wasted!"

Val was even more tired; and she said nothing.

Return to Air

The Ponds are very big, so that at one end people bathe
and at the other end they fish. Old chaps with bald
heads sit on folding stools and fish with rods and lines,
and little kids squeeze through the railings and wade
out into the water to fish with nets. But the water's
much deeper at our end of the Ponds, and that's where
we bathe. You're not allowed to bathe there unless you
can swim; but I've always been able to swim. They
used to say that was because fat floats—well, I don't
mind. They call me Sausage.

Only, I don't dive—not from any diving-board,
thank you. I have to take my glasses off to go into the

water, and I can't see without them, and I'm just not going to dive, even from the lowest diving-board, and that's that, and they stopped nagging about it long ago.

Then, this summer, they were all on to me to learn duck-diving. You're swimming on the surface of the water and suddenly you up-end yourself just like a duck and dive down deep into the water, and perhaps you swim about a bit under-water, and then come up again. I daresay ducks begin doing it soon after they're born. It's different for them.

So I was learning to duck-dive—to swim down to the bottom of the Ponds, and pick up a brick they'd throw in, and bring it up again. You practise that in case you have to rescue anyone from drowning—say, they'd sunk for the third time and gone to the bottom. Of course, they'd be bigger and heavier than a brick, but I suppose you have to begin with bricks and work up gradually to people.

The swimming-instructor said, "Sausage, I'm going to throw the brick in—" It was a brick with a bit of old white flannel round it, to make it show up under-water. "—Sausage, I'm going to throw it in, and you go *after* it—go *after* it, Sausage, and get it before it reaches the bottom and settles in the mud, or you'll never get it."

He'd made everyone come out of the water to give me a chance, and they were standing watching. I could see them blurred along the bank, and I could hear them talking and laughing; but there wasn't a sound in the water except me just treading water gently, waiting. And then I saw the brick go over my head as the instructor threw it, and there was a splash as it went into the water ahead of me; and I thought: I can't do it—my legs won't up-end this time—they feel just flabby—they'll float, but they won't up-end—they *can't* up-end—it's different for ducks . . . But while I was thinking all that, I'd taken a deep breath, and then my head really went down and my legs went up into the air—I could feel them there, just air around them, and then there was water round them, because I was going down into the water, after all. Right down into the water; straight down . . .

At first my eyes were shut, although I didn't know I'd shut them. When I did realise, I forced my eyelids up against the water to see. Because, although I can't see much without my glasses, as I've said, I don't believe anyone could see much under-water in those Ponds; so I could see as much as anyone.

The water was like a thick greeny-brown lemonade, with wispy little things moving very slowly about in it— or perhaps they were just movements of the water, not things at all; I couldn't tell. The brick had a few seconds' start of me, of course, but I could still see a whitish glimmer that must be the flannel round it: it was ahead of me, fading away into the lower water, as I moved after it.

The funny thing about swimming under-water is its being so still and quiet and shady down there, after all the air and sunlight and splashing and shouting just up above. I was shut right in by the quiet, greeny-brown water, just me alone with the brick ahead of me, both of us making towards the bottom.

The Ponds are deep, but I knew they weren't too deep; and, of course, I knew I'd enough air in my lungs from the breath I'd taken. I knew all that.

Down we went, and the lemonade-look quite went from the water, and it became just a dark blackish-brown, and you'd wonder you could see anything at all. Especially as the bit of white flannel seemed to have come off the brick by the time it reached the bottom and I'd caught up with it. The brick looked different down there, anyway, and it had already settled right into the mud—there was only one corner left sticking up. I dug into the mud with my fingers and got hold of the thing, and then I didn't think of anything except getting up again with it into the air.

Touching the bottom like that had stirred up the mud, so that I began going up through a thick cloud of it. I let myself go up—they say fat floats, you know—but I was shooting myself upwards, too. I was in a hurry.

The funny thing was, I only began to be afraid when I was going back. I suddenly thought: perhaps I've swum under-water much too far—perhaps I'll come up at the far end of the Ponds among all the fishermen and foul their lines and perhaps get a fish-hook caught in the flesh of my cheek. And all the time I was going up quite quickly, and the water was changing from brown-black to green-brown and then to bright lemonade. I could almost see the sun shining through the water, I was so near the surface. It wasn't until then that I felt really frightened: I thought I was moving much too slowly and I'd never reach the air again in time.

Never the air again . . .

Then suddenly I was at the surface—I'd exploded back from the water into the air. For a while I couldn't think of anything, and I couldn't do anything except let out the old breath I'd been holding and take a couple of fresh, quick ones, and tread water—and hang on to that brick.

Pond water was trickling down inside my nose and into my mouth, which I hate. But there was air all round and above, for me to breathe, to live.

And then I noticed they were shouting from the bank. They were cheering and shouting, "Sausage! Sausage!" and the instructor was hallooing with his hands round his mouth, and bellowing to me: "What on earth have you got there, Sausage?"

So then I turned myself properly round—I'd come up almost facing the fishermen at the other end of the Pond, but otherwise only a few feet from where I'd gone down; so that was all right. I turned round and swam to the bank and they hauled me out and gave me my glasses to have a good look at what I'd brought up from the bottom.

Because it wasn't a brick. It was just about the size and shape of one, but it was a tin—an old, old tin box with no paint left on it and all brown-black slime from the bottom of the Ponds. It was as heavy as a brick because it was full of mud. Don't get excited, as we did: there was nothing there but mud. We strained all the mud through our fingers, but there wasn't anything else there—not even a bit of old sandwich or the remains of bait. I thought there might have been, because the tin could have belonged to one of the old chaps that have always fished at the other end of the Ponds. They often bring their dinners with them in bags or tins, and they have tins for bait, too. It could have been dropped into the water at their end of the

Ponds and got moved to our end with the movement of the water. Otherwise I don't know how that tin box can have got there. Anyway, it must have been there for years and years, by the look of it. When you think, it might have stayed there for years and years longer; perhaps stayed sunk under-water for ever.

I've cleaned the tin up and I keep it on the mantel-piece at home with my coin collection in it. I had to duck-dive later for another brick, and I got it all right, without being frightened at all; but it didn't seem to matter as much as coming up with the tin. I shall keep the tin as long as I live, and I might easily live to be a hundred.

Lucky Boy

This was just about a perfect summer afternoon, with sunshine, flowers blooming, and birds singing, even to a cuckoo (only that happened to be Lucy next door, who was good at it); and it was Saturday into the bargain. Everything was in Pat's favour: jobs done, and his family safely in the back-garden. He strolled down the front-garden to the front-gate. Clicked open the gate . . .

Free . . .

And then: "Where are you going, Pat? Will you take me with you, Pat? Take me too, Pat!" The cuckoo had stopped calling, because Lucy had given up mimicry to poke her face between the slats of the dividing fence. "Take me."

If he went through the gate and on, without her, Lucy would bawl. That was understood on both sides. The question was: Would anyone from either house come in response to the bawling? And if they did, would they bother to get to the bottom of things: detain Pat for questioning, cross-examine him on his plans, ruin his perfect afternoon?

Of course, he could run for it—now, instantly. That was perhaps the only certain way of keeping his afternoon to himself. He would just leave Lucy bawling behind him. What made him hesitate was that once he used to take Lucy on expeditions even without her asking. When Lucy had been a baby in a pram, he had helped to wheel her. Later on, when she was old enough to walk, he had taken her to the sweetshop, and he had even shared his pocket-money with her. Not so very long ago he had taken her regularly to the swings and the sandpit and see-saw on the Recreation Ground.

So he paused, holding the gate open before him, to reason with her. "I'm not going where I could take you," he said, "you're too little."

But she simply repeated: "Take me."

Pat had delayed, and Lucy's mother must have been watching from the window. She opened the front-door and came down the path towards them, carrying a pair of red sandals. She had misunderstood the situation. "Lucy," she said, "you put your sandals on if you're going out of this garden." And then, to Pat, "Are you taking her to the shops or to the swings?"

Pat was going to neither, so he said nothing.

Lucy's mother went straight on: "Because if it's the shops, she can have fourpence."

"No," said Pat. "Not the shops."

"Well, then!" said Lucy's mother to Lucy. "You do as Pat tells you, now." She turned briskly back to the house. Lucy's mother was always like that.

Lucy had been putting on her sandals. Now she went through her front-gate, and waited for Pat to come through his. She held out her hand, and he took it.

They walked to the Recreation Ground, towards the swings. The sun still shone, flowers bloomed, birds sang—and Lucy with them; but the afternoon was ruined for Pat.

They were within sight of the swings. "Will you push me high?" Lucy was saying.

He made up his mind then. Instead of loosening his hold of her hand, so that she could run ahead to the swings, he tightened it. He gripped her attention. "Listen, Lucy. We could go somewhere much better than the swings." Yes, he'd take Lucy, rather than not go at all. "We'll go somewhere really exciting—but secret, Lucy, mind. Just you and me, secretly."

"Secretly?"

"Come on."

They veered abruptly from the direction of the swings and scudded along the fencing that bounded the Recreation Ground on its far side. They left behind them the swingers, the sandpit-players, and even the football-kickers. Down to the lonely end of the Recreation Ground, where Pat had poked about a good deal recently. He had poked about and found a loose fencing-stake that could be prised up and swung aside, to make a gap.

"No one's looking. Through here, Lucy—quickly. Squeeze."

Gaps in the fencing of the Recreation Ground were not unheard of; nor boys getting through them when they should not. But trespassing through such holes was disappointing. On the other side of this fence lay only a private garden. True, it ran down to the river; but what was the use of a river-bank neatly turfed and herbaceous-bordered and within spying-distance of its house? And if one tried to go further along the river-bank, one soon came to another fence, and beyond it, another private garden; and so on. Trespassing boys looked longingly over to the other side of the river, which was open country—thin pasturage, often flooded in winter, with ragged banks grown here and there with willow and alder. They looked, and then they turned back through the gap by which they had come. And in due course the Groundsman would notice the hole and stop it up.

Pat's hole had not yet been found by the Groundsman, which was a bit of luck; but beyond it, in the garden, lay—yes, *lay* was the very word—the best luck of all.

"Now," Pat said, as Lucy emerged from the hole in the fence into the garden. "Keep down behind the bushes, because of being seen from the house, and follow me. This way to the river-bank; and now—look!"

Lucy gazed, bewildered, awed. The turf of the bank had been mutilated and the flower-border smashed by a tangle of boughs and twigs that only yesterday had been the crown of an alder-tree, high as a house, that grew on the opposite bank. For years the river had been washing away at the roots of the alder, dislodging a crumb of earth here and a crumb there, and in flood-time sweeping away the looser projections of its bank. For years the alder had known that its time was coming; no roots could hold out against it. In the drowsy middle of the day, on Friday, there had been no wind, no extra water down the river; but the alder's time had come. It slid a little, toppled a little, and then fell—fell right across the river, bridging it from side to side.

The people of the house were exceedingly annoyed at the damage done to their grass and flowers. They spent the rest of Friday ringing up the farmer from whose land the alder had fallen, but the farmer wasn't going to do anything about a fallen tree until after the weekend; and *they* certainly did not intend to, they said.

They did not know about Pat. After school on Friday, he found his hole in the fence and, beyond it, the new tree-bridge to take him across to the far bank of the river.

Then, he had had no time to explore; now, he had.

"Come on!" he told Lucy, and she followed, trusting him as she always did. They forced a passage through the outer branches to the main trunk. The going was heavy and painful. Pat, because he was just ahead of Lucy, shielded her from the worst of the poking, whipping, barring branches; but still he heard from behind him little gasps of hurt or alarm. More complaint than that she would not make.

They got footholds and handholds on the main trunk, and now Pat began—still slowly and painfully—to work his way along it to the far bank. The last scramble was through the tree-roots, up-ended at the base of the trunk, like a plate on its edge. From there he dropped on to the river-bank of that unknown, long-desired country.

And now he looked back for Lucy. She had not been able to keep up with him and was still struggling along the tree-trunk, over the middle of the river. She really was too little for this kind of battling—too young; yet Pat knew she would never admit that, never consent to his leaving her behind.

As he watched her creeping along above the water, he was struck by the remembrance that Lucy could not swim. But she was not going to fall, so that did not matter. Here she was at the base of the trunk now, climbing through the tree-roots, standing beside him at last. Her face, dirtied and grazed, smiled with delight. "I liked that," she said. She put her hand in his again.

They began to move along the river-bank, going upstream. "Upstream is towards the source of the river," said Pat. "We might find it. Downstream is towards the sea."

"But I'd like to go to the sea-side," said Lucy, halting. "Let's go to the sea-side."

"No, Lucy. You don't understand. We couldn't possibly. It's much too far." He pulled her again in the upstream direction.

A ginger-coloured, puppyish dog had been watching them from one of the gardens on the other side. They noticed him now. He stared and stared at them; then gave a bark. Before Pat could prevent her, Lucy had barked back—rather well and very provocatively.

"Hush!" said Pat; but he was too late, and Lucy had barked again. The dog had cocked his head doubtfully at Lucy's first bark; at the second, he made up his mind. He began to bark shrilly and continuously and as if he would never stop. He pranced along his section of the bank, shrieking at them as they went.

"Now look what you've done!" Pat said crossly. "Somebody will hear, and guess something's up."

Lucy began to cry.

"Oh, I didn't mean it," said Pat. "No one's come yet. Stop it, do, Lucy. Please."

She stopped, changing instantly from crying to the happiest smiling. Pat ground his teeth.

The dog continued barking, but soon he could keep level with them no longer, for a garden-fence stopped him. He ran up and down the length of it, trying to get through, banging his body against it. He became demented as he saw Lucy and Pat going from him, curving away with the river-bank beyond all possible reach. They heard his barking long after they had lost sight of him.

And now the nettles began. At first only a few, but at the first sting Lucy made a fuss. Then the clumps grew larger and closer together. They might have tried skirting them altogether, by moving in an arc from the river-bank; but in that direction they would have been stopped by another stream, flowing parallel to their own, and not much narrower. They could see that very soon the nettles were filling all the space between the two streams.

Pat considered. He had foreseen the possibility of nettles that afternoon, and was wearing a long-sleeved sweater as well as jeans and socks and sandals. Lucy and Lucy's mother, of course, had foreseen nothing: Lucy was wearing a short-sleeved dress, and her legs were bare. Legs always suffered most among nettles, so Pat took off his sweater and made Lucy put it on like a pair of curiously constructed trousers, with her legs thrust through the sleeves. Then he found himself a stick and began beating a way for them both through the nettle-banks.

Whack! and *whack*! left and right, he slashed the nettle-stems close to the ground, so that they toppled on either side and before him. Then he trampled them right down, first to one side, then to the other. Then again *whack*! *whack*! and trample, trample. From behind him Lucy called: "I'd like to do that."

"Oh, I daresay!" he said scornfully.

"Aren't you coming back for me?" she asked next, for his beaten path had taken him almost out of sight. So he went back to her and took her pick-a-back for some way; then decided that didn't help much, and was too tiring anyway. He put her down, and she waited behind him while he whacked. She kept her sleeved legs close together and hugged her bare arms close round her, against the nettles.

The nettles were always there—*whack*! *whack*! and trample, trample—until suddenly they stopped. There was an overflow-channel from the river, man-made of brick and stone and cement patchings; it was spanned by a rather unnecessary bridge with a willow weeping over it. Lucy settled at once on the bridge under the willow to serve tea with leaves for plates and cups, and scrapings of moss for sandwiches, fancy cakes and jellies. She was very happy. Pat took off his sandals and socks and trod about in the thin film of water that slid from the upper river down the overflow-channel into the lower stream. He climbed about on the stone stairs down which the overflow water ran, spattering and spraying, to its new, lower level. The wateriness of it all delighted him.

Then the barking began again. There, on the other side of the river, stood the gingery dog. By what violence or cunning he had got there, it was impossible to say. It was certain, however, that he would bark at them as long as he could see them. Some loose stones were lying in the overflow and Pat picked up several and threw them at the dog. Those that did not fall short, flew wide. The dog barked steadily. Lucy left her tea-party and descended on to a slimy stone to see what was happening, and the sliminess of the stone betrayed her: she slipped and sat down in the inch of water that flowed to the lower stream, and began to cry. Pat was annoyed by her crying and because she had sat down wearing—and wetting—his sweater, and above all because of the ceaseless barking on the other bank.

He hauled Lucy to her feet: "Come *on!*"

Beyond the overflow there were fewer nettles, so that they went faster; but the gingery dog still kept pace with them, barking. But Pat could see something ahead that the dog could not: a tributary that joined the main river on the dog's side and that would check him, perhaps, more effectively than any garden fence. They drew level with the tributary-stream; they passed it;

and now they were leaving the gingery dog behind, as well as the nettles.

They entered a plantation of willows, low-lying and neglected. Saplings had been planted here long ago for the making of cricket-bats; then something had gone wrong, or perhaps the trees had been forgotten. Cricket was still played and willow bats used for it; but these particular willows, full grown and ageing, had never been felled for the purpose. So, in time, like the alder downstream, many of them had felled themselves. Ivy, which had made the plantation its own, had crept up the growing trees and shrouded the fallen ones with loose-hanging swathes of gloomy green.

Lucy was charmed with the place and would have liked to resume the tea-party interrupted under the weeping willow. Here were tree-stumps for tables, and —an improvement on the overflow—meadowsweet and figwort on the river-bank that could be picked for table-decoration. But she would not be left behind if Pat were going on.

Pat saw his chance. "I won't leave you behind," he promised, "but you can play while I just have a look ahead at the way we must go. Then I'll be back for you." Lucy accepted that. He left her choosing a tea-table.

So, for a very little while, the afternoon became as Pat had planned it: just for himself. He went on through the sad plantation and came to the end of it—a barbed wire fence beneath which it would not be too difficult to pass. Beyond lay more rough pasture. Far to the right he saw the occasional sun-flash of cars on a distant road. But he was interested only in the river.

Looking, he caught his breath anxiously, for a punt was drifting downstream. The only occupant, however, was a man who had shipped his pole in order to drift and doze in the sun; his eyes were shut, his mouth open. He would not disturb Pat and Lucy, if they did not disturb *him*.

Shading his eyes against the sun, Pat looked beyond the punt, as far as he could see upstream. The river appeared very little narrower than at the fallen alder, so probably he was still far from its source. Still the river-bank tempted him. He could see it curving away, upstream and out of sight. Even then he could mark the course of the river by the willows that grew along it. In the distance he could see the top of a building that seemed to be standing on the river; perhaps a mill of some kind, or the remains of one; perhaps a house . . .

Anyway, he would soon see for himself.

He had actually stooped to the barbed wire fencing when he remembered Lucy. Recollecting her, he had also to admit to himself a sound coming from where he had left her, and that had been going on for some time: a dog's furious barking. He sighed and turned back.

Back through the sad plantation to the part of the river-bank where he had left Lucy. "Lucy!" he called; and then he saw the dog on the opposite bank. Its gingeriness was darkened by the water and mud it had gone through in order to arrive where it was. For a wonder, it had stopped barking by the time Pat saw it. It sat there staring at Pat.

"Lucy!" Pat called, and looked round for her. There on a tree-stump were her leaf-plates, with crumbs of bark and heads of flowers; but no Lucy.

His eyes searched among the trees of the plantation, and he called repeatedly: "Lucy! Lucy! Lucy!"

There was no answer. Even the dog on the opposite bank sat silent, cocking its head at Pat's calling, as if puzzled.

It was not like Lucy to wander from where he had left her. He looked round for any sign of her beside the tea-table. He noticed where she had picked meadow-sweet and figwort; stems were freshly broken. A wasp was on the figwort. Lucy was afraid of wasps, but perhaps the wasp had not been there when she had picked what she wanted. The figwort with the wasp on it leant right over the water.

"Lucy!" Pat called again. He went on calling her name while he slowly swivelled round, scrutinising each part of the willow-plantation as he faced it. He came full circle, and was facing the river again.

The river flowed softly, slowly, but it was deep and dark. Every so often, perhaps at distances of many years, somebody drowned in it. Pat knew that.

He looked over the river to the dog and wondered how long he had been there, and why he had barked so furiously, and then stopped.

He looked at the bank where the figwort grew: it was crumbly, and now he noticed that some of it had been freshly broken away, slipping into the water.

He saw the flowing of the water, its depth and darkness. Speechless and motionless he stood there, staring.

The summer afternoon was still perfect, with sunshine, flowers blooming, birds singing, even to the cuckoo . . .

Then suddenly: *the cuckoo*! He swung round, almost

lost his balance on the edge of the river-bank, and, with a shout of "Lucy!", started off in quite the wrong direction. Then he saw a hand that lifted a curtain of ivy hanging over a fallen tree-trunk. He plunged towards it and found her. She was hiding in a green, ivy-cave, laughing at him. He pulled her out, into the open, and began smacking her bare arms, so that she screamed with pain and astonishment and anger. The dog began barking again. Pat was shouting, "You stupid little girl —stupid—stupid—stupid!"

And then another voice was added to theirs, in a bellow. The punt Pat saw earlier had come downstream as far as the plantation, and the man who had been dozing was now on his feet and shouting: "Stop that row, for God's sake! And you ought to be ashamed of yourself—beating your sister like that! Stop it, or I'll come on land and stop you myself with a vengeance!"

The two children stared, still and silent at once. Then Pat gripped Lucy and began to pull her away from the river-bank and the man and the dog. They blundered through the plantation and reached the barbed wire. They crept under it, and Pat set off again, pulling Lucy after him, across the meadows to the right, towards the distant road.

"We're going home," he said shortly, when Lucy, in tears, asked where they were going.

"But why aren't we going back by the river-bank and over the tree? I liked that."

"Because we're not. Because I say so."

When they reached the road, they turned in the direction of home. There was a good way to go, Pat knew, and Lucy was already grizzling steadily. She hated to walk when she had to walk. There was not much chance of anyone they knew stopping to give them a lift; and, if anyone did, there would be a lot of questions to be answered.

They passed a bus stop, and plodded on. Lucy was crying like a toothache. Pat heard a car coming, and it passed them. Later, a lorry; and it passed them. Then there was a heavier sound behind them on the road, and Pat turned: "Lucy, quick! Back—run back!"

"Back?"

But Pat was already dragging her with him back to the bus stop, signalling as he ran. The bus drew up for them and they climbed in and sat down. Pat was trembling. Lucy, who had needed a handkerchief for some time now, passed from sobbing to sniffing.

The conductor was standing over them. "Well?" he said.

Pat started. "Two halves to Barley," he said.

The conductor held out his hand.

Pat felt through all the contents of his trouser-pockets, but before he reached the bottoms he knew, he remembered: "I've no money."

The conductor reached up and twanged the bell of the bus and the driver slowed to a halt, although there was no bus stop. "I've a heart of gold," said the conductor, "but I've met this trick before on a Saturday afternoon."

Pat could feel the other passengers on the bus were listening intently. Their faces, all turned in his direction, were so many pale blurs to him; almost certainly he was going to cry.

The conductor said, "You've some hard luck story, no doubt, you and your little sister."

"She's not my sister," Pat muttered.

A voice from somewhere in the bus—the voice of Mrs Bovey, who lived down their road—said: "I know him. He's Pat Woods. I'll pay the fare. But what his mother would say . . ."

"You're a lucky boy, aren't you?" the conductor said.

Pat did not look at Mrs Bovey; he did not thank her; he hated her.

The conductor took Mrs Bovey's money and twanged the bell again, so that the bus moved on. He held out two tickets to Pat, but did not yet let him take them. "Latest fashion, I suppose?" he said. Pat did not know what he meant until he pointed, and then Pat realised that Lucy was still wearing his sweater as trousers.

"Take that off," Pat ordered Lucy. As she was slow, he began to drag the sweater off her.

The conductor interrupted to hand him the tickets. "You be gentle with your sister," he warned Pat; and from somewhere in the bus a passenger tutted.

"She's not my sister, I tell you."

"No," said Mrs Bovey, "and what *her* mother will say I don't like to think."

"You'll grant you're in charge of her this afternoon?" said the conductor. "Speak up, boy."

In the silence, Lucy said: "You're making him cry. I hate you. Of course, he looks after me. I'm always safe with him."

Pat had turned his head away from them—from all of them—as the tears ran down his cheeks.